DETROIT PUBLIC LIBRARY
W9-BXE-173

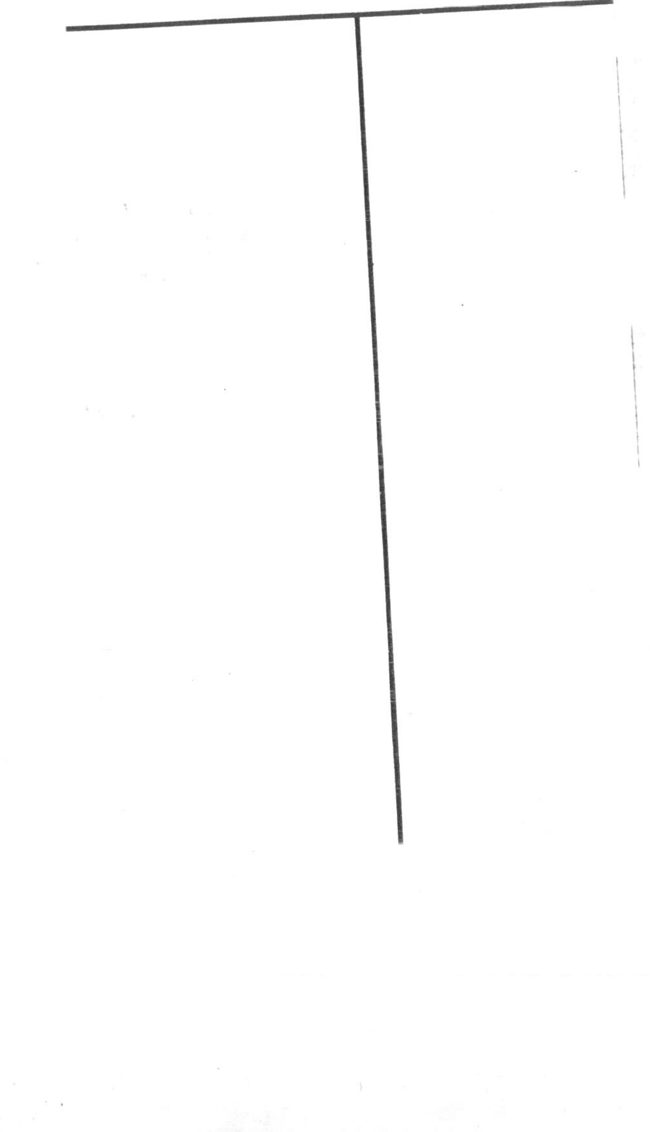

The Best of Intentions

The Best of Intentions

By Firth Haring

William Morrow and Company, Inc.

NEW YORK 1968

All of the characters and events in this novel are completely imaginary. Any resemblance to persons living or dead is purely coincidental.

Grateful acknowledgment is made to Norma Millay Ellis for permission to quote from Sonnet XL, from *Fatal Interview,* by Edna St. Vincent Millay, published by Harper & Row. Copyright 1931, 1958 by Edna St. Vincent Millay and Norma Millay Ellis.

Published simultaneously in Canada by
George J. McLeod Limited, Toronto.

Printed in the United States of America.

Library of Congress Catalog Card Number 68-26435

For my parents

The Best of Intentions

Six years after the accidental death of her only child, an idle woman develops a passionate attachment to the teen-age boy she is tutoring.

CHAPTER ONE

MARGARET BOLLINGER walked as far as the end of the north porch with her husband; there at the top of the steps leading down to the garage she kissed him and wished him a good day. She waited until the car had passed out of sight before she turned away from the balustrade. Then she walked briskly down the width of the porch, across the front of the house on the east porch, and passed from there onto the south porch where she anticipated her breakfast and where Mrs. Haskell was waiting to serve it.

"Good morning, Mrs. Haskell."

"Good morning, Mrs. Bollinger. A fine morning today."

"Couldn't be finer." Margaret pulled a chair over to the glass table and snapped open the morning paper. The two women had already said good morning once but that had been when Mrs. Haskell had poured for Mr. Bollinger. They always said it a second time, with Mrs. Haskell adding a comment on the day's weather, as if the day could not really begin until the man was out of the house.

Margaret had realized long years before that Mrs. Haskell could not be depended upon to give an accurate account of the weather. It was either a fine morning or a raw morning. As she finished her coffee and lit her first cigarette of the day, she noticed that, despite the woman's report, it was already, at a quarter past eight in the morning, hot. August hot. She picked up her sunglasses and, with thumb and index finger, pressed them on in order to scan the gardens and lawns that surrounded the house. The dew that she had noted an hour before had already disappeared. Her rambler roses struggled over the stone wall as if to escape the sun, and the otherwise long lush lawns showed through bare in spots in spite of the attention lavished upon them. The sun blazed on the river below, and the woods at the back of the house were alive with locusts, screaming out the temperature. But the house, situated as it was with its back to the wooded hill and its three terrazzo porches offering access to the river breezes, was never uncomfortable in the summer; indeed, Nyack, New York, was noted for its pleasant weather in that season.

The paper, this morning, did not hold her attention as usual, and her eyes wandered often to the great winding bridge that twisted across the river. The stream of traffic coming out of New York was heavier than usual for the morning, but it gave, she knew, only a hint of what it would be by early evening. The third and last long weekend of the summer seemed to induce a larger exodus from the city than either of the other two, as if they, the travelers, were trying to make up, at the end of the summer, for all they had meant to do at the beginning. Her eyes picked out a red convertible and followed its slow progress across the great bridge until it had disappeared into the hills fifteen hundred feet below her porch.

It was the first August in five that she had spent in the house; it was just six years ago, August 29, 1958, that the accident had happened. She did not have to force herself to recall that day, although the memory of it had not been, in the last years, a constant one. The incident, reconstructed so often, so minutely, had, in time, become crystallized in her mind so that merely to recall it, instantly evoked the whole scene; the day and the holiday traffic that had passed by for hours and hours on the state highway directly below the house. She recalled how she had waited all afternoon for John to come home and how, with each passing hour, the traffic had seemed to grow heavier. She recalled how the child, Anna, had fretted with a heat rash and been unable to sleep, and John's phone call from his cousin's house two miles down the highway to say that he was leaving the car there and walking home to save time. And then, at dusk, his "Hullo!" from the foot of the driveway. She had left the child and run down the lawn to meet him, the lawn, wet and slippery, with a breeze floating a cloud of white paper moths across it and fireflies turning into tiny sulphurous glows in the shadows. She remembered how they had embraced in full view of the passengers in the cars backed up along the road and then had started up the drive, arm in arm, toward the house. But a shout from the house had interrupted their conversation—a shout and Mrs. Haskell running along the porch waving a white towel. "Anna!" she was shouting, "Anna's fallen into the pool!" And Margaret recalled how she and John had looked at each other and, for some reason, burst out laughing. And then of how they had broken into a clumsy trot in their efforts to reach the pool; and of how, like Sisyphus, they had seemed to make no progress in their struggle up the long steep driveway. And then, finally, when they reached the poolside, Mr. Baker, the gardener, was there giving the child artificial respiration and Mrs. Haskell was rushing to and fro shouting, "Thank God! Thank the Lord! Thank the Lord he was still here." She meant Mr. Baker who, in order to take advantage of the light in pruning the spirea, had stayed past his usual quitting time. She recalled how the child's eyes had flickered open, then closed again. "The water come up," said Mrs. Haskell. "She turned all blue and then it come up out of her like a little fountain. She'll be all right now. Just thank God he was still here." And John had run off to the garages to get one of the other cars to take the child to the hospital, forgetting in the excitement, the traffic backed up bumper-to-bumper on the road.

She recalled the nightmarish trip to the hospital with Mrs. Haskell and Mr. Baker in the back seat of the car, John driving, and she in the front seat holding the child, who breathed, but whose small body still contracted with violent spasms. And she recalled how, after breaking through the holiday traffic at the foot of the driveway, they had decided to take country backroads to the hospital to avoid tie-ups, and of how, ridiculously, they had lost their way—lost their way in the very county where they had both lived all their lives. She recalled finding the road again and checking the child into the hospital, at last. And she recalled the final fact: that, despite the doctors' having given them every assurance that Anna would recover, she had died anyway, ten days later, of pneumonia.

Six years had passed. It was 1964 and she was thirty-two. The years had taken their toll on her spirit but they had left hardly a trace on her figure or her fine smooth skin. She could see a distorted image of herself in the concave side of the silver coffee pot. Her skin was as pale as five cold Augusts in the north of France could leave it, and her dark eyes, which brooded and started with her moods, contradicted the light color of her hair, which she wore parted on one side and pulled horizontally across her forehead. She had a broad, almost Slavic face, which the concavity of the coffee pot now exaggerated, high cheekbones, and a full stern mouth. She was not beautiful, but there was an expressiveness, an intelligence about her, a sober and thoroughly enchanting way she had of looking up through a screen of lashes—not coquettishly, but rather with the indolence of a sunbather, as if to save herself the effort of moving her neck muscles.

The briskness and energy that she had simulated earlier in the day for her husband's benefit had disappeared. The morning's memories had left a tiny vertical furrow between her eyebrows and, as she rose to leave the porch, she bumped into the table and sent a cup shattering on the tiles. Mrs. Haskell's head shot out briefly from the kitchen window, then disappeared. Margaret was grateful. She knew that on any other morning the woman would have pointed out that it was from the last complete set of Spode that had belonged to John's mother. Mrs. Haskell knew the house and every one of its coffee cups, pickle forks, minute salt spoons, and damask cloths better than Margaret ever would: she had been introduced to them fifteen years before Margaret had stepped foot in the house and had maintained them ever since. She knew and lamented every one of the Dresden figurines that Margaret had, upon taking up her residence, banished to the attic. "The house has never been the same since them dear little shepherds got their walkin' papers," she mourned to Mrs. Burdick, with whom she was thick. And Mrs. Burdick, who was all sympathy and ears when it came to being let in on a family secret, shook her head and said, "That's the way it is with these modren marriages."

Encouraged, Mrs. Haskell's indignation knew no bounds. "What's more," she drew out, depicting, tattling, relishing the effect, "what's more, she's took down the pictures of the old folks and put up some French lithographs instead." She rocked back on her heels to get the full impact of this shocker on Mrs. Burdick.

"That's arty for you," Mrs. Burdick had commiserated. "They'll do it every time."

Margaret placed the Spode fragments on the table and proceeded toward the east porch and the front entrance of the house. Her figure was good. She was neither tall nor elegantly built, yet she moved gracefully and even at times sensuously. She had a firm vigorous body, and the cotton sundress she wore revealed the slim hips and hollowed-out buttocks of a taller woman. She was wondering how to make up for the loss of the cup to Mrs. Haskell. There was no love lost between the two women, both mistresses, as it were, of the same house, but they got on after a fashion and managed to keep the status quo. They had only had one real falling out, and that was a year after Anna's death when Mrs. Haskell had had the shortsightedness to say to Margaret, "You better have another one. They say it helps." Margaret, who had hardly been able to believe her ears, said, after a split second of silent fury, "And you'd better mind your own business if you expect to stay on here."

Neither of them ever apologized for it, nor did either of them expect an apology, but from that day onward they treated each other with the greatest and coolest courtesy (although Margaret continued to allow her to take those small liberties which it was natural—for her—to take). The courtesy was not and never had been insincere on the part of Mrs. Haskell. She knew her breach had been an almost unforgivable one and, in thinking of the episode in retrospect, she never failed to wonder at Margaret's having kept her on. The truth of the matter was that Margaret agreed with her; another child *would* help. And they had tried for another but with no success; now, at thirty-two, she had almost lost interest in the project.

Their lives were set now. John, at forty-two, would not have much patience with a wriggling infant, and Margaret had other diversions: the piano, gardening, her correspondence, her occasional literary efforts, a friend or two, an annual visit from her niece, Marina. Another woman might have found that life confining or selfish or negative, but Margaret found her insularity sufficient. If at times it did seem to her a too egotistic life she led, she could placate her conscience with the knowledge of her little charities, the flowers she had the gardener disburse from April through October to the local nursing home and, in the summer months, the bushels of tomatoes, beans, and peaches that were delivered to the Catholic orphanage in the valley below.

Yes, the house and the gardens sufficed. She found little to interest her in the village, among the local society, or even in the city, which was so close that on a clear day she could see the towers of the tallest buildings from the top of the mountain behind the house. There were more books in the library than she could read in a lifetime and more music in the piano room than she could possibly learn. Her husband loved her, and she him, though he had grown rather duller in recent years, prematurely gray in the spirit. She had never been unfaithful to him, despite all the summers she had passed alone in France; she had never, in fact, seriously entertained the prospect of being unfaithful. He had wanted her to go this summer again to France, but she had demurred; one could not go on grieving forever. Nevertheless, this morning she had sensed his reluctance to leave her. Her kiss had been light and reassuring. "I'm all right now," it had said.

She stepped across the doorsill into the house, removed her sandals, and padded barefoot across the cool smooth floors. The rugs were still up for the summer. Only now, after ten years of marriage to John Bollinger, did the house reflect her own taste. It had taken almost that long to dispose, as decently as possible, of course, of the Victoriana that his mother had inherited from hers. John had been quite lamblike about the monstrous family portraits, but she had seen the wrench it gave him to think of parting with the homely objects among which he had grown up: the uncomfortable red plush sofas, the dark commodes and sideboards, the ornate mahogany dining table and the awkward leather armchairs. But, Margaret had prevailed; everything went but the china, the silver, the linen, a couple of Duncan Phyfe love seats, the Chippendale desks, and the beautiful silk oriental rugs, ancient and priceless. The house now suited her in every way. The light-colored walls, superseding twenty years of green, gave an impression of great spaciousness; they seemed at times almost to take on the blueness of the river far below or, in winter, the azure tinges of northern light. The translucent draperies afforded a view of the magnificent river to the east and the gardens to the north and west, and the furniture, deceptive in its delicacy, was at once attractive and comfortable.

She had come to love the house. She could spend weeks in it without once desiring to stray away. Aside from the Augusts spent in France, the extent of her activities beyond the borders of her gardens was an occasional foray into the village, her daily walk on the wood road above the house, and a dinner engagement now and then. And each November she went to her dressmaker in the city and spent a week being pinned and pleated, sashed and draped in the latest fashions. During the evenings of that week, John stayed in town too. They went each night to a concert, or the opera, or the ballet, giving Mrs. Haskell and a staff hired for the occasion the opportunity to fall-clean. The walls and ceilings and floors were vacuumed, the rugs were laid, the house was treacherous with step ladders, hoses, and pails. Window-washers, tilers, painters, puttiers, and polishers invaded the peace and privacy of Margaret's house and, at the end of the week when she returned, it was as if a new season had been ushered in during her absence. What always struck her upon her return was the unfamiliar appearance of the house without the gay striped awnings that lent it, for six months of the year, the jaunty atmosphere of a bazaar.

Despite the fact that it was a warm and friendly house, it was a "grown-ups" house. It would have been difficult to imagine a child romping through the long rooms or roller-skating across the gleaming parquet floors. And it would have been even more difficult to find a trace of a small child ever having been an occupant there; yet a pair of sharp eyes might have detected the two small screw-holes in the wall at the top of the stairs where the expandable safety gate had once been erected, and an explorer would have found in the attic a dismantled crib, an old-fashioned wicker carriage, and a faded hobby horse.

Margaret's life had not always been so solitary. Before the child's death they had been very gay. They had had many friends, they had entertained and were entertained, they were even civic-minded to a degree, and she had acted to mild acclaim in some of the productions of the local little-theater group. But their misfortune had changed all that. She had found it necessary to be alone in order to work out her grief. She blamed herself for the tragedy and shut herself in the house as if to punish herself in that way for her negligence.

As the months passed, the self-imposed solitude had become more a mercy than a punishment. In her aloneness she had turned to music, to the piano, to Bach. She had played for hours every day: fugues, rondos, the preludes, the concertos. The regular patterns, methodical progressions, orderly structures and consoling gravity of the music imposed a welcome order on the extraordinary chaos of her life and her emotions. Later, when the worst was over and the piano had done its part in her rehabilitation, she continued the habit of solitude. She continued to avoid society and, in that way, avoided *its* chaos. She resented any intrusion of it in the new peace she had eked out for herself.

Besides the music, the other aspect of her salvation had been the routine she had established and forced herself to live by. It was another means of restoring order and serenity to her life. She had existed, almost artificially, according to the demands of a set of rules; she rose at a certain hour and breakfasted at a certain hour, off certain patterned dishes. On certain days she wore certain clothes, listened to certain radio programs, took a walk at a certain time in a certain direction, planned a certain menu for dinner, and played certain pieces on the piano, at a certain hour. And, as the weeks passed, there was a certain comfort in being able to say, "Yes, I was doing this *last* Thursday at noon," and to know that there was no reason on earth why she should not expect to be doing it the next Thursday as well. Thus, she systematically went about removing the unexpected from her life. She wanted for it never again to be possible for her world to be devastated, as it had been on that August evening. A shout from the porch had once sent everything in her life that was sure and sweet and certain spinning; she was going to ensure that it did not happen again. And so it was by rules and hours set and patterns fixed that she lived. The routine was at once exhausting and delivering; in the end it saved her sanity.

Mrs. Haskell was the jealous porter who had guarded the door behind which Margaret carried out her systematic recuperation. When friends and well-wishers arrived with gifts and consolations, it was Mrs. Haskell who intercepted them on the front porch and turned them firmly away. Although this led to a certain amount of speculation in the village as to whether or not Margaret had gone off her rocker, most of the townspeople learned to honor her privacy. They left her alone, not severely, but politely, which suited her very well.

Such had been her life for six years. The house, the piano, the gardens had been enough. She had taken up gardening in the second autumn after the child's death, and it had been the first positive sign to John and Mrs. Haskell that she was recovering from her grief. It had been then that Mrs. Haskell, who made some paganistic association in her mind between gardening and generation, tulip bulbs and maternity, had uttered her ill-received remark to Margaret about trying for another baby.

If the gardens came to represent to Margaret a fertility she could not achieve within herself . . . if they did, well, there was no harm in it. At any rate, she was almost always to be found in the cool of the morning or on fine evenings when the sun had only just begun to sink behind the mountain on one or another of the seven terraces, spraying, watering, hoeing, or simply on her knees weeding. She stayed there until the last rosy spike on the river glistening far below had faded and left her in obscurity on her hillside.

Now, as she walked through the series of rooms leading to the music room, she could see through the west windows the beloved gardens. Terrace upon terrace, ascending toward the hill they sprang, until, at the foot of the hill, they ended in a profusion of wisteria and bleeding heart and the hill took over: a tangle of ivies, an unruliness of forgotten myrtle and trumpet vine, of drooping hemlock and birch, of honeysuckle and sumac. But even in *that* confusion, there was some order; the slates that formed the path from the driveway up through the terraces continued in an elongated S through the vines and up, up the hillside to the "wood road," a graveled track hacked out of the eastern face of the mountain. It was that path that Margaret took in the fall and winter, when the vines had died and it was accessible: up the path, a scramble over the white guard rail on the road, and a mile or two in either direction, with the chance of meeting anyone as rare as it is of meeting a stranger in one's own kitchen garden. The terrace idea had been John's. It had come to him with the filling in of the pool after the child's death. Filled in and planted with roses, the pool had only seemed more apparent than ever. So he and a landscape architect friend designed a plan for six more terraces in the hope that they would disguise and diminish in importance the original one. The plan had been highly successful.

She sat at the piano, opened her book to a Mozart aria she was learning, and began to play. It was already ten in the morning; she had spent an hour longer over breakfast than usual, Mrs. Haskell noticed. She played and played. The house rang and echoed with her music. The piano was tonally excellent, and to Mrs. Haskell's untrained ears Margaret played flawlessly. The whitewashed stone walls of the kitchen fairly vibrated with arpeggios, the window panes tingled with grace notes and Mrs. Haskell, overcome by the eloquence of it all, threw out her chest, opened her mouth, and let loose. She sang as if her heart would break. She went through all the motions of delivering a resounding aria. She darted to and fro about the kitchen as if explaining her role to a spellbound audience; she beat on her chest, she wrung a dish towel, she dashed the back of her wrist across her forehead, baring her teeth and glaring violently into the face of an invisible Papageno. She sang magnificently, poignantly, unforgettably. But she sang silently for she could not, as she often said of herself, carry a tune in a bucket. When the aria was over and she had brought down the house, as she did every morning, taken her bows and given an encore or two, she put away the towel and plugged in the iron. An hour later Margaret caught sight of her trundling the teacart down the south porch and past the windows on the east to the corner where she, Margaret, always had her lunch.

Broiled trout (because it was Friday and Margaret had been Catholic too long to dispense with fish just because the Pope had), sliced tomato, still warm from the garden, long tender green beans and a glass of Chablis, cold and dry. Though Margaret was Catholic, Mrs. Haskell had once observed, "You'd never know; it's only the fish gives it away." She ate, slowly and meditatively, gazing out from time to time over the wide, swiftly flowing river and the curving bridge. The traffic had stepped up a little since the morning. She sighed, poured the hot black coffee, and lit a French cigarette, the best part of the meal. The smoke curled up, blue and slow, then eddied at the corner of the house and swirled quickly out of sight. From the gardens she caught a whiff of lemon verbena and leaf mold. Two wrens chased each other excitedly across the lawns—lawns the violent green of well-watered grass—and vermilion geraniums nodded in a border by the hedge. All was well in her world.

She narrowed her eyes and looked past the lawns again away out over the water, recalling what the river had looked like before the bridge had been built. Unhampered by the silver girdle that spanned it now, it had swung, free and swift and wide, on its course below the Palisades. But the bridge had changed it, had changed in fact not only the river, but the whole county, for in connecting it to the city, it had laid a path for the real-estate men, the developers, the promoters, the operators, the sharks, the get-rich-quick men who had thundered over it in hearty packs, bringing the new ideas of the new America to the farmlands of the fertile county. Over the river, up the mountain, down into the valley and across the rolling fields they had left their trail; whole villages mushroomed in what half a year before had been a gallant orchard. Shopping centers, low and restive, parking lots, laundromats, cinemascopic screens crouching in once sweet-smelling meadows, flashing motels, restaurants orange and blue and unavoidable, discotheques, teen-agers' "night clubs," Robert Hall, Dairy Queen, Frosty Freeze, Stop and Bowl, thruways, parkways . . . a whole new world. She had been in love with it once, but she had let it go by the board, a lover who hadn't lived up to expectations.

She frowned and closed her eyes and with her fingers traced the S of the bridge along the base of the wine glass. Lunch was over and the afternoon lay ahead. "What shall I do? What shall I do with the day?" she asked herself. "Withaday, Withaday, Withaday," echoed the cars as they hummed off the bridge and into the tunnel of trees.

"Shall I work in the gardens?" Heat waves in their special limbo shimmered and discouraged.

"I've played the piano. Shall I read?" But her mind was primed with her own thoughts and she did not require another's.

"Perhaps I should go to church." But that was inconvenient. It had been a long time since she had gone and to go now would mean driving to another town where the priests would not recognize her. In the village they would expect an explanation for her long absence, and that would mean confession, with the priest behind the grille breathing hard from the heat, and penance, then communion, which would mean returning on Sunday, and absolution. It would be better to say a Hail, Mary, here on the porch—it was as peaceful as a church—and be done with it. She missed a phrase at the end, however, and had to start over again. And the second time she fumbled at the same spot and gave it up as a bad idea.

"Why don't you come home, John?" She looked at her watch. It was only three and he'd said half-past four. She searched in her pockets, found an emery board and idly filed her nails. A factory whistle wailed briefly in the village, signifying closing time. She moved across the porch to the glider, out of the sun. A clock somewhere in the house chimed once for the half hour. She picked up a copy of Verlaine—

> *"Comme un vol criard d'oiseaux en émoi,*
> *Tous mes souvenirs s'abattent sur moi,*
> *S'abattent parmi le feuillage jaune*
> *De mon coeur . . ."*

and dropped it again onto the glass-topped table. John, are you coming?

At four she could shower and dress. She pumped the glider, as if to urge the hour on.

Suddenly, without warning, there was a terrific explosion. It was as if a bomb had gone off in the next room. A window shattered somewhere in the house. The blast echoed and re-echoed off the mountain and the mountain groaned and let slip a bit of itself. The earth and rock slid, spilling faster and faster, down its side. Margaret, stunned for an instant, leaped to her feet. She moved tremblingly to clutch the porch railing and reached it just in time to see the gardener romping down the terraces, dragging his rake behind him and casting his eyes over his shoulder at every third step, as if he expected the whole mountain to avalanche on top of him.

"Gawdamighty, what was that?" he bawled, bolting over an azalea hedge and hurtling up the porch steps. For a moment, Margaret had the fleeting impression that he was going to throw his arms around her.

"What *was* that, Miz Bollinger. What was it?" He pranced about the porch, wild-eyed with fear.

"I think," she said faintly, "I think it must have been a jet breaking the sound barrier."

Mrs. Haskell pounded through the house and out onto the porch, breathless and, for once, speechless. She opened her mouth, as if to sound an alarm, then shut it again at the sight of the gardener. "A jet!" he roared, flailing his arms at her. "It was only a jet."

"A jet?" Mrs. Haskell looked indignant and a little injured, as if miffed that the explosion had *not* indicated the end of the world.

"Yes, Mrs. Haskell, I think so," said Margaret wearily. "I think it was only a jet. Did I hear a window go?"

Mrs. Haskell pulled herself up, gave the gardener a look that plainly said, "And what, pray tell, are you doing mucking up the front porch in them boots?" and stalked into the house to see about the window.

"Exasperating idiots," thought Margaret as the gardener lurched away. Her heart was still beating wildly as she returned to the glider. "What a thing to have happen. Today of all days." She tried to relax but it was impossible. She left, weak-kneed, to bathe.

It was not until she lay in her bath that she saw the comedy of it. Of the two explosions, one that six years before had shattered her life, the other that had shattered only her window, the second had for a moment seemed the more significant. In some ways it was, for coming as it had on the anniversary of the first, it helped her to complete her break with the other. Shock treatment to hasten the analysis. She remembered how the hood on the black Lincoln that was carrying them from the funeral to the cemetery had flown up suddenly, right in the middle of Main Street, and how she had heard her cousins in the car behind burst out laughing. She hadn't been able to laugh then, but now . . . she lay back in the bubbles and smiled broadly. And when, still smiling, she stepped out of the bath and into her room, John was there lying on the bed. He sat up and dried off her back with a corner of the bedspread.

"Mrs. Haskell said you heard the jet."

"It was terrifyingly loud."

"I know. I heard it too, a half-hour ago across the river."

"I thought the world had come to an end." She kissed him. "Thank you for coming home earlier, darling."

He patted her head, ruffled up her hair in the back. It would have been a fine time to make love, but John seemed tired and, besides, he was apt to think it crude, on the anniversary.

❋ CHAPTER TWO ❋

An hour later found them on the porch sipping vermouth. The sun had already slipped behind the mountain and now threw its final glory on the river. Tiny waves, gold and red, bobbled mysteriously, enticing the gulls to swoop and fall upon them. "Do you notice," she asked herself, "how the gulls, circling and diving, supply the vertical and parabolic movement to the dominant horizontal thrust of the river?" She did not bother to reply to her own rhetoric; instead, she watched the traffic on the bridge, which was heavy now, but moving freely. A sailboat, jaunty with its striped sail, veered in close to the bridge as if to tantalize the carbound travelers. In another hour, when they had finished with dinner and returned to the veranda with coffee and cigarettes, the scene had changed. The river was dark except for the streaming snakelike bridge, and the evening had grown violent with the August rasp of katydids.

The phone rang in the house. Once. Twice. It was cut short the third time. Mrs. Haskell thudded toward them through the house. "It's for Mrs. Bollinger," she said in a voice charged with significance. Margaret rose reluctantly and went into the house.

"It takes nerve, if you ask me."

John, who had thought he was alone, was startled. "What?"

"I said it takes nerve," repeated Mrs. Haskell softly behind him. "That was Mae Baker."

"Who?"

"Mae Baker. And tonight, too." She disappeared with a flip of her apron.

"Who is Mae Baker?" he wondered. "Baker. Baker, the gardener. His wife perhaps?" He shrugged, pumped thoughtfully on his pipe and tried to catch something of his wife's conversation. A firefly floated past in the darkness. He swiped at it unsuccessfully and smiled at his bad aim. It floated imperturbably away over the porch railing and into a hydrangea bush. Katydids had terrorized the snoring tree toads into inaudibility; thunder rumbled, and a flash of heat lightning lit up the eastern sky, revealing briefly the river flecked with whitecaps. The violence and tension of the night pleased him, safe as he was on his own porch. He heard Margaret's step and turned to greet her as she approached. She touched his outstretched hand in the darkness and sank down beside him on the glider.

They sat in silence until he recalled why she had left him.

"Who's Mae Baker?"

"How did you know it was Mae Baker?" Her voice had an edge to it.

"The omniscient Mrs. H."

He could sense her displeasure. "Mae Baker is Ralph Baker's widow."

"That's what I thought." He took a puff on his pipe, trying to figure it out. Had she called on the anniversary of her husband's unfruitful heroism to condole with them? "What on earth did she want?" he asked finally, and then, as he felt her gathering her anger, regretted that he had not dropped the subject.

"She wanted me to do her a favor." There was an unkindness in her voice that he had seldom heard before.

He did not ask her to explain, but his every sense was attuned to her distress. He was waiting for the crack in her voice, the movement of her hands, the unbridled laughter that would signal the breakdown he had been expecting for six years. He waited but she gave no sign and he began to feel that she wanted to be asked to explain. He reached for her in the darkness and gently stroked the back of her neck. She jerked her head out of his reach. "She had the brass to ask me to tutor her son in French," she blurted angrily.

He was relieved, not so much at the nature of Mrs. Baker's request, which he did not care about, but because she seemed to be out of danger of losing control of herself. "Well," he said soothingly. "Well, now, that's not so bad."

"Not so bad! Of course it's not so bad, tutoring him. What's bad is her calling tonight."

"Now, Margaret . . ."

"Now, Margaret." She mimicked him bitterly. "As if I would refuse! Of course I'll tutor him. But to call tonight, as if it were to be a payment . . . and after the payment they *did* get, then." He recalled the "payment." After Baker's resuscitation of Anna, they had given him, in gratitude, and before, a week before Anna's death, a sum that had seemed, even to them, extravagant.

"Now, Margaret," he said again. "Don't get upset about it. It's highly improbable that she remembers the date."

"I bet. Besides, I could swear she'd had a few."

"Do you know her son?" he asked, to divert her.

"Oh, I vaguely remember him. He used to come here with his father." But he could see that she was not interested in the boy.

He persisted. "How old is he now?"

"I don't know. He must be about fourteen. Fifteen, at the most, I guess."

He was rather pleased, on the whole, with the idea. It would be something for her to do. Something to think about, to plan the week around, or at least a day or two in the week. "How often will you have him?"

"I suppose once a week. It depends on how bad he is."

Her idleness had always disturbed him, for he did not see in either her piano playing or her gardening productivity enough to make life gratifying. He had thought once of adopting a child in order to give her something to do. But when he had suggested it to her, she had been hurt. "Don't you think I'll be able to have another of my own?" He apologized and never mentioned it again. Other women in her situation might have dissipated themselves, and there had been times, when the prospect of having another child diminished, that he had worried about this. But he had underestimated her will, her control, her ability to discipline herself. The life she had made for herself had apparently been enough; *he* had been enough. His little successes had sufficed her; she had not needed successes of her own. And so in time he had grown accustomed to her strange lethargy, although he had never liked it. He had never been able to quite cast off the conviction that she would be happier if she had some humanitarian work to do. He had urged her to work for the Red Cross as his mother had done so well, or to volunteer at the hospital, but she had laughed at him. "And who would run the house and look after the garden? And who would be here when you got home at night? I'm fine. Leave me alone."

And now, this fine chance had come along to educate, to cultivate, a young mind. He regarded it as a stroke of luck and was even benevolent enough to attribute it to Mrs. Baker's kindly nature. "She probably *does* remember the date and probably even that it's Margaret's first August here since then," he said to himself. "She thought it would give Margaret something to think about. It was very thoughtful of her. It was a generous, tactful gesture."

Mae Baker turned the corner of Broadway and River Street. It was already quarter past six. Leave it to Pottsworth to think of a letter he had to get in the late mail on Friday afternoon, and the Friday before Labor Day too. A little black dog darted out from behind someone's privet hedge and rushed at her ankles. She threatened it with her handbag. It retreated into the hedge and yapped at her as she continued on down the hill. "Damned mutt. I'll put some poison out for him one of these days and then we'll see who's so smart." She kicked open the gate of Mrs. Watkins' picket fence and glanced up at the windows on the second floor. They were closed. "How many times have I told him to open them windows if it don't look like rain. Crap!" She gave her thigh a good whack with her handbag. "What's the use of talking? He takes after his old man for being lazy." She thrust her key savagely into the lock and entered the house. The air, trapped in the stairwell all day, smacked her in the face. "Good and hot too." She grimaced, climbed the flight leading to the apartment she shared with her son, opened the door, crossed the room, and threw open the window. A river breeze, cool and sprightly, rushed into the room. "And if he'd a thought of that two hours ago it would have been decent in here by now." She mopped her brow, kicked off her shoes, and went into the kitchen to pour herself a drink. "Deserve it on a Friday. Taking his guff all week." She was speaking now of her employer, Mr. George Pottsworth, a kind, honest, generous, well-respected citizen who ran a small establishment called the South County Feed & Grain Company and whose secretary she was.

She went to the refrigerator, gin in hand, for ice cubes. The ice trays were empty. She set her glass down on the table so firmly that some of the gin splashed onto the oil cloth and uttered a most unladylike expletive. "I'll knock his teeth down his throat if he don't learn to follow directions." She filled the trays with water and shoved them into the freezing compartment, added a little water to her gin, and padded back to the living room where she stretched herself out full-length upon the sofa. She sighed as contentedly as it was possible for her to sigh and flexed her calf muscles luxuriously. It was the best part of the day, to come home and relax. "I like to go home," she once confided to a friend. "There I can take off my shoes and scratch and burp when I please and nobody to give me a look."

But home. It was some home. She cast her eye derisively around the dreary little room, taking in the dingy, fly-specked wallpaper, the shabby rug, the rural landscape that one of her nieces had assiduously painted (failing, however, to quite cover the guide numbers), the limp curtain at the room's one window. Even the dusty knickknack shelf made a poor showing with its bronze baby shoe, the Etruscan vase made in Japan, the mottoed chamber pot, and the miniature china sombrero that Leroy had given her one Mother's Day. It had been home for five years, or since the untimely death of her husband had made her the breadwinner of the little family. She recalled the advertisement for the apartment in the local paper: "Sunny 3½. River view. Quiet. Cool." It was sunny, yes, between two and three in the afternoon when a single sunbeam stole in an insufficient arc across the room, picking out the frayed spots in the rug and impaling upon itself the dust particles that hung in the air. The apartment included, besides the living room (which metamorphosed at night into her bedroom), the kitchen, bathroom, and a proper bedroom inhabited by the man of the house. She groaned and shifted her weight at the thought of him. As for "river view," a glimpse of the Hudson was certainly possible if one cared to risk one's neck by leaning out to catch it. And yes, she would agree that it was cool, in the winter, and quiet, if you were lucky, between one and six in the morning. She groaned again, drank deeply of her gin and water, and reached in back to undo what she referred to as her harness. This seemed to give her some relief, for a smile temporarily improved her features, or perhaps it was the effect of the gin flowing through her system, anaesthetizing.

Mrs. Baker was not always so ill-humored as she was on this hot afternoon. She could come on as quite a lady when she wanted to, and she had managed to convey the impression at her office that she was a cut above the rest of the personnel, and to be treated accordingly. She had overwhelmed Mr. Pottsworth, the clerk, the typist, and the stock boys from the start with her airs. Mr. Pottsworth, who considered himself fortunate to have her (and thus treated her well) would have been astonished to discover the ill will she bore him. It was only after she had left the office that she indulged in the luxuries of temperament and sloth. "I'd be a happy woman," she often sighed to herself, "if only I was my own boss."

And there had been a time, too, when she had been her own boss; when she had gotten her hands, at last, on the drowning money that the Bollingers had given her husband. He, the fool, had gone haywire, having his hands on a little cash for the first time in his life. Went straight out and bought a motorboat (he'd always wanted one); then overcome with misgivings at his rashness, had refused to buy insurance for it. Of course, as anyone could have told him, it was smashed to smithereens in the first hurricane that came along. In her rage and his remorse at this unhappy event, the rest of the money had been entrusted to her management. And she did with it exactly what she had always wanted to do; she opened a secretarial school and called it "Miss Sterling's Business Classes." Sterling was her mother's maiden name. "It's got class," she told her husband when he asked who the hell Miss Sterling was.

She rented two rooms in a brand-new office building on Main Street, advertised in the local paper, ordered reams of paper, some of it printed with "Miss Sterling's Business Classes" (the printer, unfortunately, left the second *s* off Miss), ordered shorthand textbooks, myriad other office supplies, a dozen desks ("for a start"), and a telephone, and waited for the students to apply. But none did. She waited for a whole summer. Every morning for three months she went to the rented rooms and waited. When the phone rang, she would wait until it had rung at least twice before she answered—to show the caller that she was in no hurry. But if it weren't her husband, or Leroy, or a wrong number, it would be Mrs. Watkins wanting to talk. "I must go now, Betty," she would say after a while. "Someone may be trying to get through." After three months, her husband upped and died and she'd had to give up the rooms. The textbooks even now yellowed in the basement of the River Street house. The remainder of the drowning money, now only half of the original sum, had since been gathering interest in the First National Bank and Trust Company. It was to be, as she and her son both knew, for his "college education."

"The trouble with a hick town like this," Mrs. Baker said scornfully, "is that the poor girls go into the ribbon factory, the rich ones go to college, and the ones in the middle have big ideas and have to go to New York City to some fancy Business Training Institute. Small town's not good enough."

"You should have thought of that before you started," her son remarked. He had an answer for everything.

Mrs. Baker sat up, polished off her gin, and returned to the kitchen for another nip. She kept the bottle carefully hidden at the back of the broom closet. Back on the sofa once more, she put her feet up and turned her attention to her son. She was an ambitious woman and her chief ambition was that he should rise in the world, as much to glorify herself as him. Discarding the possibility of receiving an inheritance or another windfall like the drowning money as too far-fetched, she had hit upon a "college education" as the best means to this end. Her problem was how, in her circumstances, she would be able to send him to college. The drowning money was clearly not going to be enough. It would do for a year, perhaps for two if he would work, but she wanted him to go for more than a year or two. She pulled thoughtfully on a hair that sprouted from her chin. Unfortunately, he had not shown much inclination for working and thus the little cache at the First National had not noticeably increased. He had spent the summer as a counselor at a fancy boys' camp in Vermont. The salary he had received had been a mere token but she had wanted him to go. "It'll give you a good chance to see how the other half lives," she told him.

When he returned, she asked him for his wages so that she could deposit it in their account. "I spent it all," said he, lighting a cigarette. She was so charmed by this, having never seen him smoke before, and so impressed by the casual, yet debonair attitude he struck in doing so, that she forgave him on the spot for spending the money. When she brought up the subject again, just as they were sitting down for supper that night, he diverted her by assisting her so gracefully and unassumingly into her chair that she resolved, when she recalled hours later what she had started to say, never to mention it again. "If he's learnt to be a gentleman this summer, that's enough for me," she said to Mrs. Watkins.

But that was a week ago and now, as she sat in the gathering dusk in her shabby room, she began to think that perhaps it wasn't enough. "Why should I work my fingers to the bone to send his highness to a fancy school?" she muttered. "Why don't he get a job? Why don't he get good marks so he could get a scholarship?" The answers to these purely rhetorical questions were quite clear, even to this loving mother.

Gloom followed her as she propelled herself toward the kitchen and the evening meal. She unlocked a can of sardines, poured the oil into the sink, and slapped the fish on a slice of whole wheat. She ate in a thoughtful, trance-like silence. When she had finished, she split a peach in two and ate it, standing over the kitchen sink. "And where is he?" she muttered. "I'd like to know. Big Time Charlie can keep all hours." She flung the peach stone out of the window where it landed on a corrugated tin garage roof and rolled merrily down into the gutter. "And me a poor widow." She dissolved in tears and, clasping her arms about herself and turning her streaming face beseechingly toward heaven, she went rocking to and fro across the kitchen moaning comforting phrases to herself.

When she had lost interest in this entertainment, dried her face, and returned to the sofa, an idea occurred to her. "Mrs. High and Mighty Bollinger. She's so smart going off to parlay-voo every summer. If she gave him French lessons maybe he *would* get a scholarship." Her ingenuity pleased her and, striking what she imagined was the pose of a grande dame, she strutted across the room, nodding haughtily, graciously, condescendingly, depending on each passer-by. "And how do you *do,* my dear. It's been simply ages since I've seen you. Oh, my son? Oh, my dear, wouldn't you know! He's up on the hill again. At the Bollingers', of course. They dote on him. Can't see enough of him. He's always up there, every time you turn around. They chat away for hours and hours. What do they chat in? Oh, French. What else?"

Mrs. Baker of River Street turned in her tracks, fists clenched. "Why, they owe it to him," she said fiercely. "The rich ought to help the poor."

This last seemed so true to her, so everlastingly just, that she dropped to her knees in front of the telephone directory and began to flip through it in search of the Bollingers' number.

"And that's not the only reason they owe it to him," crowed she to herself. "They owe it to him because his brave, loving father saved their baby's life."

She found the number and scribbled it down on the cover of the book. She struggled to her feet, red in the face and rather moist here and there from her exertions. "And I don't mind if I pour meself a little snort just to celebrate," she said aloud. "I deserve that much."

In late August, dusk falls quickly and early, harboring lovers, and others. A young couple picked their way down the side of the mountain toward the place near the road where their car was parked. Ralph Leroy Baker, Jr., stepped down heavily on a rotten branch that lay across his path. The branch snapped under his weight causing him to twist his ankle. He swore. "Not again, I hope," tittered his friend with a sly poke in the direction of his ribs.

He limped after her and grabbed her wrist. She did not resist him as he pushed her against a tree and thrust his hand inside her blouse. "Since when, not again?"

She did not answer. She merely sighed, her lips parted, and shifted her weight dreamily. He withdrew his hand abruptly and gave her a friendly shove. "Not again, you hope. Ha!"

"Ralph!"

"Come on. It's too late."

She followed him. They stumbled in the dusk to the car at the foot of the hill. He did not open the door for her; she would have burst out laughing if he had. "Lah de dah tonight!"

"Take me for a Dairy Queen," she begged as he started the motor.

"No, it's too late I told you."

"Oh, please."

"No. Didn't your old man tell you to get the car back early for once?" The car lurched and started forward. She pouted becomingly. "Pffft."

He ignored her and headed for the town.

"You never do anything I wanna do."

"Pipe down. I'm thinking." They drove in silence to River Street where he braked the car and got out. "See ya round, doll." She sullenly shifted over to the wheel.

"So long, sport," she said. And off she drove.

He climbed the stairs to the apartment and let himself in with his own key. He did not see his mother at first, for she had not yet turned on the lights and the apartment was dark. Her voice revealed her presence to him.

"Fine time to be getting home, isn't it? I had a nice meal all cooked."

"Sorry." He snapped on the overhead light. She sat, her stockinged feet propped on the coffee table, watching him. "Sorry! I bet you are."

"I said I was sorry. I'll eat it cold."

"Oh, no you won't. You'll eat a can of sardines . . . and be glad of it."

The prospect offended his sensibilities. "I'm not hungry anyway."

"Delicate," she sneered. "How delicate. Mr. Fancy Pants won't eat sardines."

He could tell by now that she had been drinking. He walked past her and into his room.

"Fancy Pants!" she roared after him.

He shut the door and turned on his radio to drown her out. Then he went to the mirror to examine the place where the girl had bitten him. It was already turning blue and ugly. "Damn her." He studied his face appraisingly and not without satisfaction. He had the good looks of a clean-cut American male of seventeen, yet there were certain subtle variations that differentiated him and made him infinitely more attractive. He was one of those fortunate young men who was never embarrassed by sudden and radical bursts of height. He was well-knit, well-proportioned. His limbs had grown in accordance with his torso and his complexion had never inconvenienced him. It was as fine and smooth as a baby's and dusky now after his summer in the sun. His eyes were dark and shrewd and wise beyond their years and his nose differed from the usual by the presence of a small exciting irregularity at its bridge. The rest was true to type: a straight brow, a cropped head, slightly on the small side, good ears, and a sensuous mouth, usually insolent, at times truculent.

His insolence and his scorn were abundant. He was scornful of his living parent, his dead parent, the apartment, the town, his teachers, the girls he knew—in short, the sum of his background and environment. He had two ambitions: to rise above his present status in life and to win somehow the respect and admiration of his male contemporaries. He had never experienced any difficulty in arousing admiration in the opposite sex.

No one had ever called him an intellectual; he was by no means, however, unintelligent. What he lacked in brain power he made up for in shrewdness, a powerful intuition, and a certain charming and convincing way he had of lying. He was intelligent enough to know what he wanted. He was ambitious enough to make sure he got it.

He lit a cigarette and lay across the bed. The tiny room was stifling and the smoke he exhaled hung gray and heavy in the air. From the window he could look down into the backyards of the five or six neighboring houses: straggling back stoops, unpainted fences, dilapidated dog coops. Unwashed children played kick-the-can in the darkness, and their mothers, having gathered for their evening gossip, slapped at mosquitoes and called sporadically and unmusically for their children to come home. "Why am I here?" he thought, as he had thought a thousand times before. "I'm not a part of this. When will I be able to get away from it?"

He flipped the cigarette out the window and rolled over on his back. He flicked off the radio impatiently and something in that act brought to mind the girl he had been with that afternoon. He touched the welt on his neck and swore softly. He could hear, through the thin walls, his mother moving about in the other room. He would have to open the door soon, he knew, or roast to death. Just as he was about to get up, she called him.

"Le—roy?"

"Yeah?"

He opened the door. He could see immediately that her mood had changed. She flinched at the expression on his face which quite clearly failed to convey any good will.

"I have some news," she said timidly.

"Yeah?" There was not the slightest trace of enthusiasm in that syllable.

Determined to out with it, she crossed the room and arranged herself in an arm chair. "Why don't you sit down?"

He sat on the arm of the sofa, grudging her even that much attention.

She grew angry at his nonchalance. "If you don't want to hear it, I'm not begging you."

"I'm listening. What more do you want?"

"You *could* act a little interested."

"I'm all ears."

That would have to do. She was about to burst with her news.

"You have a tutor!" she cried joyously, pronouncing it to rhyme with scooter.

"A what?"

"A tooter!"

He grasped the idea and turned it over in his mind for a moment.

"So that's good news?"

"A tooter," she repeated. "You'll get good marks; you'll get a scholarship. See?"

His eyes narrowed. "So what am I being tooted in?" he asked cautiously.

"French." She breathed the word reverently. "French."

"French." He repeated it softly. She was disappointed in his reaction.

"Do you like it?"

"Like what?"

"The idea."

"Yeah. It's swell. Is that all?"

"Well, you don't act it."

"How do you want me to act?"

"You could ask a few questions?"

He sighed. "Where, when, who?"

"Up on the hill." She pointed with a thumb toward the mountain. "With," she paused dramatically, "Mrs. Margaret Bollinger!"

He mulled this over. "I thought she was bugs," he said finally.

"Naah! She's a little eccentric, that's all."

"Same thing, isn't it?"

"Ralph Leroy Baker." She moved toward him wagging

her index finger. "What do you care if she is? Maybe she's nuts enough to do something for you someday."

"Did I say I wasn't going to? It doesn't matter to me one way or the other."

She had expected more resistance and had prepared herself to meet it, so, although she subsided like a surprised soufflé at his docility, she could not help adding tersely, "She owes it to you, Leroy."

"How so?"

"Your father was a hero," she said proudly and sternly. "He saved her baby's life."

"Some hero. The kid died."

"Not from drowning it didn't. Your father was a hero. It was in all the papers."

"Big deal," he muttered, swinging his legs over the arm of the chair.

"What?"

"I said I'm going out. Don't hold your breath."

The door slammed behind him. She could hear him taking the stairs three at a time. "You could give some people the moon and they'd act like they had it coming to them," she said aloud.

He was glad to leave her and to leave the apartment that he so loathed. The night was cool with a breeze from the east. He plucked a piece of hedge leaf and bit on it as he started down the hill toward the river. The idea of being tutored by Mrs. Bollinger was not disagreeable to him. On the contrary, he had, now, as he neared the river, a sense of elation. He spit out the bitter leaf and bolted over the sea wall, landing on all fours on the wet sand below. He picked himself up and walked south toward the great bridge, stopping now and then to skip a piece of slate out over the water. The tiny lights glimmering from the big houses up on the hill were visible to him, and he wondered which house was hers. He could recall being taken there as a child by his father, and this memory made him recall as well his awe and uneasiness at being there amid such exotica as lemon trees and pink tiles to walk upon, and fluttering organdy. He recalled the woman who had one day offered him a spicey cookie and a frosty glass of green "Kool-Aid." (He had said, "Thanks for the bugjuice," but she had laughed and said, "It's Kool-Aid.") He recalled how, alarmed and uncomfortable, he had stayed by his father's side at first and how his father had urged him to explore. "Go ahead, Ralph, go play over there by the hill." But he had hung his head and murmured, "I'll stay here," and made a cat's cradle with a piece of string. And he remembered how one day the woman who had given him the Kool-Aid had said, "Did you ever pick tomatoes?"

And shyly, he had had to shake his head. "No."

"Well, come on, then. There's plenty ripe."

Together they had climbed the hill to the vegetable garden directly in back of the house. "Leave a little stem when you break them off," she had commanded. "Like this."

He had felt at ease with her at once. There was something in the way she stooped and huffed and puffed and mopped her forehead and talked to herself as she worked that was familiar to him. She was of his world and he could chatter away to her without restraint. And he recalled how, when they had got the basket full, she had told him to sit in the shade of the tree. He obeyed her and waited while she disappeared into the house to return with a glass of milk. He hated milk but he had drunk it, to please her, because she was his friend. But he had wondered at the same time why she had not invited him into her house. On the way home he had asked his father that and his father had answered, "You can't go in there. I work for them." The boy had accepted his father's logic. It became for him a precept, a part of the code of life he was learning. It was another rule that was not to be challenged, like not drinking river water because it was dirty.

He flushed now at the memory of a servant's snub and at himself for having instinctively picked a servant as a friend. He wondered what had become of the woman. He stopped walking to light a cigarette. The trees on the bank behind the sea wall threw their shadows across the deserted beach.

Mrs. Bollinger. He remembered her as a pretty lady who wore a dress with puffy sleeves and shoes that showed her toes. He remembered that one day he had come upon her dancing by herself on the veranda, whirling round and round and laughing aloud. She had stopped abruptly at the unexpected sight of a dark head and a pair of wide eyes observing her with interest from behind a hydrangea bush. "Well, hel-lo! Who are you?"

He had scampered away and spent the rest of the afternoon hiding behind the back wheel of his father's truck. He remembered the laughter that followed him as he ran away.

The late summer moon, a bright copper in the midnight blue of the sky, floated above him, high and free, passing unhampered over the water to the mountain. He followed it with his eyes as it moved on its way westward across his world, a world he saw as divided into those who had and those who hadn't, and where he had early learned that he was among the latter. How long would it be before he could leave that hated world behind him? As he toiled along the black and white beach, he knew that a break, a chance, a means, a possibility of leaving it, of beginning to realize his ambitions, had come along. This knowledge did not overwhelm him. He had always known that some day things would change. "Patience," sang a little wheel in his head. "Patience;

one thing leads to another." One thing was sure. He had his chance. He wasn't going to blow it the way his father had.

He was coming now to a section of the beach upon which the local gentry had built their houses. Several of his school friends lived in these houses: unpleasant, Fescennine boys whom he adored and emulated in manners, attitudes, and dress. He had known them always. He had gone all the way through school with them, but he had never been quite a part of them. *They* were friends with each other because their mothers were friends and because their fathers all commuted on the same trains to and from the city. Nevertheless, he considered them, in his deepest heart, his friends, although he was keenly aware of (and even strictly respected) the differences that separated them. They were his friends to this extent; he could take his lunch to the table where they took theirs and be welcomed by them with a hilarious shout. He could be let in on the meaning of their current obscenities and the esoteric paraphernalia of their language. He could take out the same girls; he could walk down the hill after school with them. He could go to bars and local dives with them. But that was it. He could not claim friendship through the Dartmouth alumni association, nor through the local country club, nor through adjoining property, nor shared summers, nor even through the church, for they were Episcopalian and he Baptist. Their friendship ended at the corner of Broadway and the ignominious River Street where he turned off and where they continued, to the southern end of town. With them, sex had always been his drawing card. Since the third grade he had titillated them with his jokes and stories. For years he had supplied them with food for many a feculent dream. But at the same time, he put them off. His cynicism offended them, for they were still romantic; his stories stretched their credulity. Privately they thought him dirty; privately they thought he lied. Together, publicly, they touted him, but he sensed their private thoughts, and it depressed him.

He walked now, close to the sea wall where the shadows protected him from anyone from the houses who might be taking the air on his dock. He remembered once having come to this same spot on the beach to watch a party, the summer before. He had heard the orchestra a mile up the beach. He had crept along the sea wall and lurked in a clump of bushes and drunk in the sight. The dock decorated with gay festoons, the Japanese lanterns rocking in the trees, the laughter and chatter, the sound of quick footsteps on wood over water, the women in thin summer dresses, the dazzling white of dinner jackets; he was enchanted and had crouched there in the wet sand for hours. He had been startled once by the light hushed voice of the mother of one of the boys who had come out along the sea wall to kiss a man who he knew was not her husband. When he had heard them drift off into the woods, he had stood, his eyes just clearing the wall, and watched them separate and return to the house, each by a different route.

But tonight, all was quiet in that neighborhood. "They must all be away for the weekend," he thought, "or at a party on the hill." The night was so still that he could hear the faint lapping of the tiny waves against the dock piles. He was overcome with nostalgia for that other night, for the laughter and the music, the soft lights and the festive garlands. "Where have they all gone?" he wondered. "If *I* lived here . . ." He felt slightly deserted, as if he had been invited to a grand affair and had gotten the date wrong.

There was nothing to do but to go back to River Street.

⁂ CHAPTER THREE ⁂

THE long Labor Day weekend passed and it was September. School reopened and the boy was glad. It meant that his life no longer had to revolve around River Street, as it necessarily did on the long useless days of summer.

He had received a letter from Mrs. Bollinger.

It was arranged that he was to start his lessons with her in the middle of the month, after he had seen about his school schedule. He had kept the letter, which was written on thick, creamy stationery, so thick that it was impossible to sharpen the crease where she had folded it, and took it out from time to time to examine the texture of the paper and the crispness of its corners. He admired, too, the square, bold, confident handwriting. She used black ink and had signed herself "Margaret R. Bollinger." He wondered if the initial stood for her middle or her maiden name and asked his mother, who said, "I think she was one of those Reeds from West Point. Hot stuff."

He smiled to himself.

"What's so funny?" she asked, but he didn't bother to let her in on the joke.

The lessons were to be held on Wednesdays from four o'clock until six. On the first Wednesday, he left the school at half past three and started along the road leading to her house, a distance of about two miles. The school football team was gathering on the field for daily practice. He recognized several of the boys, one doing calisthenics, another trotting around the track, two others passing a ball between them. He waved to one and got a brief nod in return. He was not athletic. There was something of the coward in him that prevented him from taking part in the rough and dangerous sport. He hated the sight of the ball hurtling at him, hated knowing that it was up to him to catch it and to carry it down the field through the enemy, the fierce tacklers. There was something, too, of the fop in him that found repugnant the sweat, the bulky, ill-fitting uniforms, the odors of the locker room, the possibility of getting an eye blackened or a tooth knocked out.

He played tennis on the school team in the spring and played well, for he was graceful and light on his feet. Furthermore, he had a keen interest in the game; he had heard it called a gentleman's sport.

Although the day was warm, there was the hint of an autumnal tingle in the air, a briskness and a clarity that seemed to lend themselves to anyone's purpose. Clusters of girls emerged from the front gate of the school. As he passed the group ahead of him, the girls rustled and preened. "There he goes, Elinor," said one of them in a mincing voice. "Say hello, Elinor." He glanced at them curiously as he passed and recognized the mortified Elinor as a freshman who had been staring at him all week in study hall with large, adoring eyes.

He soon forgot the girls. As he climbed the hill, a wider and wider expanse of the river was revealed. "Even the river looks good from up here," he thought, recalling the oily water from the foot of River Street, the refuse-strewn beach, the smell of dead fish at low tide. And the town, too, looked different from the hill; one had the impression of a quaint country village nestling in a green valley along the Palisades. One noticed the white church spires, the gleaming granite post office, the trim high school, the neat rows of houses. One did not see the squalor of the Negro section, the shoddy plate-glass storefronts along Main Street, the back yards where grass refused to grow, the concrete playground in the town park.

A car passed him. In it was a couple he knew from school on their way up the mountain. They did not see him, so absorbed were they in each other and in the anticipation of the favorite after-school sport of the high-school couples. Another car, a convertible with four boys in it, passed and slowed down.

"Lift?"

He waved them on. "Not going far." They roared off. He did not want to arrive at the lesson too early on the first day. He had timed it carefully so as to arrive a few minutes before four. The great white house came into view—first the tiled roof, then the striped awnings, green and white, then the long French windows, the porches, the gardens. But if he imagined that he saw a slender figure dancing alone across the porches with arms and face lifted to an unseen partner, he was mistaken; Margaret lay on a blue divan in her bedroom, fast asleep.

She had simply forgotten that he was coming.

He climbed the driveway, his heart beating wildly at the thought that he was to come to this grand place, and be welcome, once a week for a whole year. He would see it in three different seasons. He would become familiar with it, with its sounds: the chime of its clocks, the wind in its chimneys, the creak of its stairs under the weight of a certain step (for he had already begun to think of her step, indeed, of her, as having a certainty for him) .

He went up the porch steps and walked carefully across the pink terrazzo. He rang the bell and waited. No step approached. He rang again and turned discreetly away, so that when she came to the door she would not find him trying to peer inside.

The pealing of the door chime disturbed Margaret's sleep. She stirred uneasily but did not wake. Mrs. Haskell, downstairs in the cold cellar, also heard the bell. "Now that's him," she muttered. She dropped a few late onions into her basket and started toward the stairs. "Right on time too. Always are when they're getting something for nothing."

She set her basket on the kitchen table and started through the rooms to the front door. Although she had not laid eyes on him in more than ten years, she remembered him. She also remembered the story she had heard about him in the village only a year before, a story that had rippled for a week up and down the aisles of the A. & P., a story about his having been caught with a girl up on the mountain. The only thing that had saved him, it was said, was that the girl had just celebrated her eighteenth birthday. She walked softly so as to take him by surprise if she could. She saw him, a casual, rather elegant fellow, hands in pockets, leaning against a pillar. "Makin' himself right at home, I see."

"Why the hell don't they answer the bell?" he said to himself. "Did she forget I was coming?" He gave the pillar a little kick with the toe of his shoe and was about to turn to ring the bell a third time when he was startled by a rough voice.

"Was it you ringing the bell?"

He jumped and flushed furiously, turning toward the voice. He stared at the woman, taking in her angry face, her head done up in a red scarf, her fleshy exposed arms, her hands on her hips. She could see the resemblance between the young man and the skinny, big-eyed child, scared of his own shadow, who had come to the house years ago with Baker, the gardener.

"I'm—I'm sorry, ma'am," he stammered, wondering how the slim, pretty thing he remembered from his childhood could have changed so drastically in a decade. He decided that it must have been her sorrow. "I hope I didn't disturb you."

She waited silently for him to make the ridiculous blunder that she had suddenly realized he would make.

"I'm Leroy Baker," he said helplessly. "I'm to have French lessons with you."

She smiled ever so faintly. "Not with me," she said softly. "I'm the housekeeper here."

He flushed again, cursing to himself.

"I'll tell Mrs. Bollinger," she said. "You can wait here." And she disappeared as quietly as she had come.

So, he was still denied entrance to this damned house. His face burned with her insult. He was unable to admit, even to himself, that his mortification was more at having mistaken her for Mrs. Bollinger than at having to wait, like a peddler, outside the door.

Mrs. Haskell climbed laboriously up the stairs. "I'm not getting any younger, all these stairs." She was red in the face and puffing hard when she pushed open the bedroom door. She stood for a moment to catch her breath and to watch the second Mrs. Bollinger sleeping peacefully on the blue chaise. Flat on her stomach, with one arm pillowing her head and her feet pigeon-toeing, she could have passed for an exhausted, athletic adolescent. Mrs. Haskell was overwhelmed, briefly, with a tenderness for the lady of the house. "Baby. Tuckered out."

"It's ten past four," she said in a loud voice.

Margaret murmured something to the phantoms in her dream.

"It's ten past four," repeated Mrs. Haskell. "Leroy Baker's here."

Margaret stirred clumsily and raised herself on her elbow. She stared half-blindly around the room, searching for what had waked her.

"I said, Leroy Baker's here."

"Oh." Margaret sat up. "Who?"

"Leroy Baker."

"Oh! My schoolboy! I fell asleep! Was today the day?" She pushed a twist of hair behind her ear and sat up. She wore nothing but a half slip. Mrs. Haskell turned modestly away. "He's on the porch," she said stiffly.

"Well, tell him to come in. Isn't it warm out there?"

"He said he wanted to stay outside."

"Oh." She moved across the room to her closet. "Why on earth didn't you wake me?" She pulled a dress on over her head. "Poor boy. Not a very propitious start."

But Mrs. Haskell didn't answer. She was already halfway down the stairs.

When she had left him, Leroy, shattered by the insult, fuming with rage, had sunk down onto the glider. "These people. They own the earth." He spat savagely over the porch railing, the spittle landing on a branch of an evergreen tree. He was pleased at first and then a thought occurred to him. "My God, if she sees it there!" He got up, glanced around furtively and tiptoed across the porch to the tree. By leaning far out over the railing, he could just grasp the tip of the branch. He shook it vigorously until the blob dropped off onto a lower branch, which was impossible for him to reach from the porch. "Well, at least it's out of sight from up here." He gave it one last shake.

"Be careful. There's a bird's nest in that tree."

He whirled around and saw the woman watching him through narrowed eyes.

"S—sorry," he stammered.

"Mrs. Bollinger is coming," she said shortly. "You can wait."

She disappeared and he was left again, still outside the house. He hardly dared to move for fear she would suddenly reappear. He strained his ears for a sound of his tutor but the house was silent except for a ticking clock and an uncertain rustle now and then of wind brushing through the curtains.

He waited and waited, scarcely breathing, yet aware of his heart's beating. Finally he heard a light step. He heard her pause at the foot of the stairs. She came quickly across the floor to him and burst onto the porch, her hand outstretched, smiling. In the moment before she reached him, he took her in. Nothing escaped him: not her high bosom nor her trim flanks, not her slender, tanned legs nor her sturdy shoulders, not the sensuous curve of her mouth and her cheekbones nor the soft loop of her honey hair, not the fading slash on the side of her face nor the large black velvet pupils of her eyes.

She was upon him, it seemed, in a crush of laughter and cologne. "I'm so sorry," she said. "Did you wait long? I fell asleep." This gave her reason for more laughter. "I forgot you were coming, isn't that silly? Come into the house, don't you think? It's hot out here." She preceded him to the door and he did not fail to notice the free and sensuous way she had of walking. She wore a simple sleeveless dress of some blue material, which struck him as odd. Somehow he hadn't thought she would wear anything so ordinary. She opened the door and stood aside to let him pass. His eyes, useless at first from the effects of the bright September sun, began to dilate slowly. Objects took on form, then color, then perspective: the dark swoop of a grand piano, the blue-green of a

Chinese vase, the flutter of a sheer summer curtain over the back of a pale couch.

He felt dizzy and tottered slightly. He reached out to grasp something and it was her arm that sustained him. "Here!" She laughed and again he was aware of her perfume. "Here, this way. You're sun-blind." She led him as she would have a doddering grandparent across the cool, darkened rooms into a stone room, whitewashed and green where ivy clung to the walls. A parakeet, brilliant blue, startled by their sudden entrance, rose from a clump of fern and flew insanely about the room.

"Shush! Shoo!"

She pushed him gently toward a flowered chair. "Sit there. Are you all right?"

He sank into the chair and nodded, still feeling faint. She laughed again. She found him very humorous, indeed.

He looked at her now, curiously, and wondered what the hell she was finding so amusing. She lay back in her chair, opposite him, with her feet, which he noticed with a shock were bare, resting on a marble-topped coffee table. "A big boy like you nearly fainting. What next?" Then, "Mrs. Haskell, bring some iced tea," she shouted, alarming him.

"It must be the sun," he murmured, feeling weak all over again.

"How old are you anyway?"

"Seventeen."

"Oh." She was surprised. "I'd imagined you were younger."

"I'll be eighteen in the spring."

"Yes, I suppose that's right. I keep forgetting this is your last year. Well!" She swung her legs off the table and sat up briskly. "I thought we'd start off by simply getting acquainted. I want to find out first how much you know."

"I've had three years," he said.

"Three." She wrote the number 3 on a piece of paper and traced over it and over it from top to bottom and bottom to top. "I suppose, then, you're mostly concerned with perfecting your pronunciation?"

"No, grammar. I'm weakest in grammar."

She wrote the word "grammar" on her pad, then separated the syllables with a hyphen, which she then blackened, conscientiously.

A clink of ice cubes heralded Mrs. Haskell, who set the tray on the marble table and, picking up a glass in each hand, thrust them simultaneously at her mistress and the boy. She could not bear to serve him first, but neither could she serve Margaret first and risk being corrected by her in front of him. She left a plate of dry white crackers behind.

"If you don't care for these—Egyptian—there are others."

"I've never had them."

"Oh! well, do."

The biscuit flaked and broke when he bit into it. She pretended not to notice.

"What sort of grades do you get?"

"Fair," he said, with his mouth full.

"Your mother says you want to go to college next year."

"I've applied." He spoke incoherently again, from washing the biscuit down with tea, and named a small, obstreperous men's school in New England.

"And what do you plan to take up?"

He set down his glass and took a deep breath. "I think," he coughed pretentiously, "I think I'll do a sort of liberal arts course. I want to improve myself, see," he said earnestly. "And there's so much I want to learn. I feel I've only begun to acquire a little knowledge. . . ." Even *he* cringed at his nonsense.

She was appalled at his naïveté: to *improve* himself! "Well," she said, a little helplessly. "That's very worthy and mature of you." On her paper she had traced, he could see, the words Egypt, fair, college, John. Finally, she put away the paper and leaned forward to the table for her cigarettes. As she did so, her dress fell open at the top and he could not help noticing that she was wearing nothing underneath and that her bosom, what he could see of it, was not bad. She looked up just then and found him looking at her. She straightened up, lit her cigarette, and said mildly, "How are your irregular verbs?"

He looked her straight in the eye. "Not bad."

She flushed and stood. "Fine. That's fine."

He stood. She was just an inch or two shorter than he.

"I suggest we read a novel aloud, stopping to analyze any constructions you don't understand," she said. She went on in this didactic tone, spelling out her study plan, outlining the autumn in chapters. Their text was to have been *Le Rouge et le Noir,* but something, perhaps the way he had frisked her with his eyes on the porch, made her suggest *The Charterhouse of Parma* instead, though she had always thought it a dreadful bore. Nevertheless, she didn't want to put any ideas in his head and then find herself having to cope with a latter-day Julien Sorel. She told him to buy a notebook for listing unfamiliar words. As she spoke, she moved slowly toward the back, the west end, of the room. "And I'll expect you at four a week from today." There was something in her voice that set him on guard. He noticed suddenly a door he had not seen before. She opened it and stood aside for him to leave. He was being shown the door—the back door. Stumbling and awkward, he bobbed his head, his idea of a bow. "Thank you very much, Mrs. Bollinger. Thank you very much for trying . . . for . . . for helping me." He backed away from her, bobbing his head the while. "Thank you. My mother thanks you, too." He bumped into a table; a vase on it wobbled precariously but did not tip. She said something that in his confusion he did not hear. Somehow, he managed to get out the door and down the steps. (Later, he thought she had said, "Mind the table.") As he hurried around the back of the house, he caught a glimpse of the housekeeper at the kitchen window. Her eyelids flickered down just as he looked up.

Margaret waited until she was sure he had passed around the house and out of sight before she went out to the porch. She moved absently across the rooms, stopping once to look at herself in a mirror. She ran her thumb over her mouth. She had forgotten to put on any lipstick. She stopped again to trail her finger along a treble octave on the piano.

There was a good breeze on the porch. The river below, ancient and ageless, bloomed roseate in the dying sun. "What a queer child," she thought. She stood at a corner of the veranda and watched a red-sailed lightning veer and come about and settle itself again on a new tack. She stood on tiptoe and looked far down the driveway on the chance of seeing the confusion of a dark-eyed waif in a lilac bush. But the lawns were altogether deserted. "And not a child really, either." She thought of the look he had given her and then suddenly and stubbornly refused to think of it *as* a look. "He's as innocent as day," she mused. "Seventeen. My God, he's a baby." And yet, and yet, there was something else. She couldn't quite think what. There had been something. She sifted carefully through the catalog of impressions in her mind as one searches for a grain of sand among ten thousand, discarding one, then another. Was it this. . . . Was it that? Was it his breaking the cracker and stuffing it into his mouth when he thought I wasn't looking? Had it to do with my dress opening, after all? Or was it simply something I dreamt before he came? Ah, no! She remembered it again: "It *was* the way he looked at me on the porch, when I first came down. The way a man looks . . . as if he has a right to know . . . and not missing anything, either."

Then, "I'm bats," she thought. "It wasn't anything at all. Except in my imagination." She reached out over the railing and stripped a floppy twig of hemlock of its needles. "How queer it must be, to be seventeen! And what an odd, shambling, clumsy boy he is, first almost fainting, then tripping over his own feet!" She dusted off her hands and hurried in to dress for dinner.

She sat waist deep in the bathtub and let the reaction she had so carefully controlled at the moment of his bold look finally find expression in the train of her thought. His look had pleased her, excited her even. She liked the idea of his having seen her pretty bosom, even though his oblique comment, "Not bad," had irked her, and still did. She had married John because his approval of her had been thorough. There was no qualifying "not bad" in *his* admiration. He had found her perfect, had called her his ideal, and she had loved it, his praise, his tireless eulogizing, and had loved him for it. She had even come to agree with him. No wonder she was cross at Leroy for "not bad." She wondered idly whether he would think about her, perhaps dream about her. She submerged herself, then rose again to a perpendicular position. The water rushed off her shoulders and breasts, leaving her as gleaming and fresh as a girl. "Sixteen years ago I was sixteen." She lifted a long slender leg out of the water and examined it critically. No weak muscles, no broken veins; it was sleek and firm. She twisted the ankle around and noted the high arch and curving instep. "What have sixteen years done to me. Where have I aged?" She hadn't aged three per cent and she knew it. In another sixteen years she would be a comfortable, robust American matron, beyond care, beyond caring. But at thirty-two she was at her best. She stood and watched the water course down her slim body. She dried herself, drew on silk underwear, and went into her room. The curtains were drawn. She lay on the bed.

At sixteen she had been, as is not uncommon in girls of that age, a virgin. At seventeen, she had dabbled and digressed. At eighteen, she was a bitter, cynical, cold, and unforgiving young woman. She remained bitter, cynical, cold, unforgiving and chaste for four years. Then she married John, who never for a moment suspected that she had ever been anything but chaste.

She thought now of her seventeenth summer and of the devastating young man. She had spent the summer on her parents' farm at the northern end of the county. It was the summer her sister Julia had come home to have her baby. Although it was called a farm, its only crops were timothy and daisies, Queen Anne's lace and black-eyed Susans, butterfly weed and buffalo grass. She loved the place, every blade of grass, every grasshopper and dragonfly, every birch glen, every hummock and hillock. But after that summer it had never been the same. She remembered the first time she had seen him. Very early one hot June morning she had wandered barefoot and still in her nightgown down the stairs and out of the house. Dreamily she moved across the lawn and over the fields, splashed absently across the little brook and found herself in the cool, dark, fragrant woods. She trailed along the familiar footpath deeper and deeper into the silent woods, then took a fork and wandered southward on the bias toward the Donnelley farm. The path was firm under her feet and as clean as hard-packed earth can be. She came this same way every day, every afternoon when the sun was hottest; came to sit on the stone wall that separated the two farms and to gaze out dreamily over the neighboring fields toward the distant blue hills, dreaming of life and what little of its mysteries she knew.

But that morning a grunting and splashing, such as of some cumbersome prehistoric beast, interrupted the train of her thought. Startled, she stood poised, ready to flee back along the path should the ominous sounds grow more so. But they did not, so she picked her way along the stone wall in their direction. About a hundred yards further along, the Donnelley house and the Donnelley swimming pool came into view. And in the Donnelly swimming pool was the source of the splashing and grunting; a fishlike creature surged furiously from one end of it to the other. She watched, fascinated. Each time it came to the end of the pool, it bashed blindly into the wall and then surged off again as if enraged at the impediment to its progress. It was obviously some primitive small-brained beast for experience did not teach it that the wall would always be there. Suddenly it stopped its violent thrashing. A sleek dark head surfaced, and the boy hoisted himself gracefully onto the apron—a tall, lean, tanned, marvelous boy, wearing a pair of short, white marvelous trunks. She watched him carefully and breathlessly, on guard lest he should suddenly whirl around and dash across the lawn and into the trees and seize her. She watched him intently, admiring his nearly naked body. He was very pleasing indeed. After he had dried his legs and knocked the water out of his ears, he left the poolside and walked away toward the house. She vaguely recalled her mother saying something about the Donnelley farm being rented for the summer to some people from New York.

After that, she rose every morning with the sun, dressed quickly, and flew over the fields and through the woods to watch him. But one morning he wasn't there. She settled down on the wall to wait for him, tolerant and patient as women in love are at the first signs of their lovers' aberrations. She poked in the grass for four-leaf clovers, glancing up now and then for a sign of his approach.

"So!" It was a vigorous voice, a shout of triumph. It nearly knocked her off the wall.

Weak-kneed, she was powerless to run away. He approached. A sudden spurt of adrenalin gave her the energy to turn. "Oh, no, you don't!" He sprang forward and seized her wrist. At eighteen he was strong, stronger than he would ever be again in his life.

She struggled in his grasp. "Let me go." She was close to tears

"Spy."

"I—I'm sorry. It's my father's land."

"Does that give you any right to spy on people?"

"I wasn't spying."

"No, you were just *looking.* Suppose I was swimming naked?"

"I wouldn't have watched, then." She felt faint again.

"Not much. You'd bring all your friends with you, wouldn't you?"

"N—no. I don't have any."

"It's not hard to see why." He dropped her arm. "Well, I suppose I might as well introduce my fascinating self. My name's Teddy."

She bobbed her head gratefully. "Margaret Reed," she said. "I'm sorry."

"Well, don't give us a curtsey."

"No." She wasn't sure what he meant.

She could hardly tear her eyes from him. What a glorious thing he was! He was going to be a sophomore at Yale in the fall, he told her, and he was trying to make the swimming team.

"Now, I don't want you to come here any more and watch me. It makes me nervous, understand?"

She nodded mutely, ready to understand anything he wanted her to.

"You can come later, after I've had my breakfast. Say, ten o'clock. O.K.?"

From nine to twelve were her hours for practicing the piano. "Couldn't I come in the afternoon instead?"

"No. I work on my tennis in the afternoon."

"Always?" It sounded impertinent.

"Yes," he said firmly.

"All right." She wondered briefly how this schedule change would be received at home, but only briefly. At seventeen, there are no obstacles to accommodating one's beloved.

Someone once said that the course of true love never runs smooth. After that glorious young male had breathed a few soft words into her astonished ear and uttered one or another promise of celestial proportions and persuaded her to take off her clothes and dally awhile, and then in September had gone bravely off to Yale, promising the moon, and then had never so much as sent her a postcard, Margaret tended to agree. She came to agree even with the poet who had said:

> "You loved me not at all, but let it go;
> I loved you more than life, but let it be."

She had let it go and let it be for four years, and then forever.

After dinner they sat on the porch in their usual pacific silence, smoking. The September evening was cool; dark had risen from the earth by half-past seven. She shivered and pulled her sweater around her. The afternoon's memories still lingered; the lean laughing boy of her girlhood was caught in her mind's eye. Only a good night's sleep would release him.

"Oh! The Baker boy. Did he come?"

"Yes." It was almost as if he had sensed her thoughts and seen an analogy that she had not yet admitted to herself. The

Baker boy, he had called him. That suited him somehow.

"I almost forgot today was the big day." He was annoyed at himself for having forgotten. He supposed that the tutoring arrangement was important to her, that she was disappointed in him for having let it slip his mind.

"Big day." She echoed, and smiled at him because she knew the tutoring business was important to him.

"How was it?" He was all enthusiasm.

"We didn't do much today." After a pause, she added. "Actually, I forgot he was coming and fell asleep."

"Oh, Margaret." He was disappointed in her.

She laughed. "Poor thing. He had to wait."

"I bet he appreciated that. How old is he, by the way?"

"Seventeen."

"Oh! I didn't realize he was *that* old."

"Tempus fugit."

"Don't fall in love with him now, will you?" They laughed.

She stood. "I'm going in." He stood too and followed her.

"What's he like?"

"Who?"

"The Baker boy! You have a remarkable attention span, you know."

"He's like seventeen like," she said. "A wise guy. Do you feel like chess?"

"Gin?"

"For a nickel a point." She was good at it.

They played until he ran out of change.

Leroy had pride, lots of it, but he intended to go back to the house again, despite her snub. "Screw her," he said to himself as he left. "She may have money, but she'll go down as fast as anybody if she wants it bad enough. That's probably what she's got in mind anyway. Not wearing any underwear." He would go back because he wanted what she could give him, enough French to do well on the boards, and he was willing to put up with her arrogance to get it. Besides, there was something else she could give him, a certain cachet that he felt was indispensable to his success in life and that he believed he would acquire if he spent enough time near her. It was a cachet born of Chippendale and Sarouk, of Turkish cigarettes and Egyptian tea biscuits, of Waterford crystal and Schumacher silk, and of so much else. "Besides," he said to himself, "if you behave, she'll throw the goodies in on the side."

As Margaret was rising from her bath, Leroy was turning the corner of Highland and Main, proceeding down the hill toward River Street and home. The idea of home seemed particularly odious to him this evening, and so, as he was not in a hurry to get there, he lingered along the way, pausing at the town's three haberdashers' windows. The first was a chain store: gabardine trousers and rayon shirts, teal blue, iridescent, and glossy stripes. He smiled scornfully at a plaster-of-paris figure who proffered six shiny rep neckties on an outstretched arm. The second shop, ancient and spotless and good, displayed decorously its autumnal flannel, its useful button-down-the-front knitted vests, and a selection of sedate ties. He took in the cordovans and noted the fine dullness of the leather passport cases. He moved on thoughtfully to the third shop at the corner of Main and Broadway, The College Shop.

For a quarter of an hour he studied the window: the soft, heathery pullovers, the smart tweeds, the sealskin belts, imported from France, the striped and plaid wool scarves, banners of an unfamiliar, coveted world, knotted casually and correctly about the throats of fine young plaster men. He closed his eyes and imagined that world. He lounged in a spacious Gothic ivied and sun-dappled window seat speaking in low tones to the young men at his feet of poetry modern and music Gregorian, of astronomy and, occasionally (respectfully, but knowingly) of heather-sweatered, silken-haired young women. From his window he saw the long English car, black and sleek, roll up the drive. Inside, in the back seat, was Margaret. "Someone from home come to drive me out to lunch," he explained gravely as he knotted his handwoven tie and adjusted his good gray jacket.

When he opened his eyes the street lights were on, although there was still plenty of daylight. He left the window and walked regretfully toward River Street. That night in bed he dwelt upon a scene in which Margaret crawled to him along a brick corridor to the pallet where he lay waiting, kissed his feet with little nibbling kisses and then made love to him. "Not bad," he said. "Do that again." He elaborated on this scene and others like it every night for a week. Always Margaret was the suppliant—he the master, unmoved, unmoving.

❋ CHAPTER FOUR ❋

Mrs. Baker banged and thumped away with the iron at one of his shirts. Every Saturday morning there were six shirts to do up: three white, two blue, one plaid. He was quite a dude, her son, having six shirts (three white). And particular about how they looked, too. She steered the tip of the iron around the buttons, careful not to snip any off. She set down the iron and whisked the last shirt off the board, draped it over a wire hanger, and thrust it into his closet. Then she remembered what she had neglected to do. She swore softly. He liked to have the collars buttoned down, he said. Otherwise they sagged, he said. She buttoned all twelve of the tiny buttons with her plump fingers. "There!" She wiped her brow with the hem of her apron. It was hot in the closet.

She returned to the board to thump at his trousers along the creases. "He should save these for Wednesday," she thought, holding up his best twill pair. Wednesday. She smiled with a mother's fondness for the woman who could do for her son what she herself could not do. She had done the last thing she could do for him, she had put him into the hands of a woman who could help him get on. She could do no more. He had gone beyond her grasp. She sighed and set the iron on the sink to cool. Across the way she could see Mrs. Brady pushing her wash out along the line. Every Saturday the wash. Mrs. Brady jerked her head in greeting but could not call good morning for her mouth was full of clothespins. Mrs. Baker waved, sighed for her sister's lot and her own, and turned from the window. She opened a can of Campbell's chicken gumbo and stuck a piece of bread in the toaster. "Where is he now?" she wondered. "He should be working. He should have a little job to help me out. He should be saving money for college. Instead, what is he doing? Where is he? Joy riding with a carload of his pals, no doubt."

Leroy was joy riding with a carload of his pals. It was a convertible, there were seven of them in it. They had been riding for an hour. The car was blue, the skies were blue. They had never been bluer, as Stuart, the most poetic of them, had just observed. It was reason enough for them all, including the driver, to look up at the sky. Not a cloud was to be seen. September blue, making the lakes a deeper blue than they were in any one of the other eleven months. The car veered, causing a sedate Chevrolet containing a fine American family of four to veer too, in the other direction. "Those crazy kids," muttered the father of the family. "They ought to be working instead of tearing up the taxpayers' roads."

"And endangering our lives," mourned the mother, twisting round to jot down the license number on a pad she always carried in expectation of such occasions. "Look, they're out of sight already." Junior and sister nudged each other in the back seat and snorted with silent laughter, glad that the daring young men had eluded their mother.

The convertible spun up the highway. The river broke

through the trees and disappeared and broke again. A flying carpet of swallows threw a shadow over them and passed, a shadow over Stuart, Christopher, Jonathan, Gray, Ted, Cornelius, and Leroy. The swift-passing shadow drew them together and shot a shiver up the spine of each one of them, though none of them would have admitted it. Christopher did say, "Take it easy, Jon," but in saying it, he ostracized himself from their communion. Nothing could make Leroy happier than to careen along so carelessly with the six young men whose six sets of parents each owned one of the houses, the delightfully cogitable, much-guessed-at river-front houses. Christopher's warning, so unnecessary, added to his sense of well-being, for there was no doubt that with it Christopher had fallen temporarily from favor. Christopher less favored than he! The probable temporariness of it did not diminish his contentment. He glanced covertly around the car. There was no sign, no telling mark, that distinguished him, set him apart, from the others. Indeed, there was a remarkable resemblance among them. He was one of them. He dressed like them, he was learning to talk like them (and, since they talked with the intonations of their fashionable mothers, nothing could be more worth learning), and he was going to college, just like them. According to his calculations, in ten years no one would be able to guess that there was a River Street in his past. This thought, each time it occurred to him, filled him with immense pride and impatience.

They were hungry, and Jonathan pulled in at a roadside joint. They trooped in and sat down with a great scraping and clatter and swagger. Christopher, in an effort to redeem himself, shoved a dollar's worth of quarters into the juke-box.

Joviality reigned. They were brothers all. The waiter, who had a wooden leg and a torso twisted from years of limping, approached. "Mushroom pizza, sausage pizza." He scribbled it on a dirty pad. "Anchovy pizza. Sorry, can't serve you beer. Underage. Cokes. Pepsi. Tab. 7-Up. Et cetera." They reached for their wallets and produced false draft cards, purchased for two dollars apiece at a Times Square arcade. Jonathan, of the seven, lacked one. "O.K., what'll it be? Schlitz, Bud, Bud."

"Two Millers here" (the champagne of beers), said Leroy loudly, daringly. They looked at him with admiration. Jonathan was grateful not to have to settle for a Coke. The waiter shrugged and wrote it down. The cops never checked in the middle of the day, and they were good customers. He replaced the pad under the belt of his trousers and swung off with his peculiar caneless roll-pump of a walk. After a while, Gray brought up their favorite topic of conversation.

"Get much last night, Teddy bear?"

"You know Arlene." They all guffawed. They knew Arlene.

"Get much last night, Leroy?"

"Tonight's the night." It was a new girl. He'd only taken her out once.

"What's the matter? Losing your touch?"

"I think she's got principles," he said. "Her father's a sky pilot."

The pizza came. They lifted out their wedges expertly. "Get much last night, Jonny, baby?"

"Not off hand," he said, and they all guffawed again.

"How come *you're* so interested, Gray?" They all stopped eating to watch him as he furnished his gaping mouth with a wedge of pizza. With his downy cheeks, sunburnt beak, and blonde head, he looked like a hungry gosling.

"Who were you out with?" asked Leroy.

"Someone you know."

"Sandra?"

"Yeah, man."

"Get in her drawers?"

"What do you think?"

"Sandra's hot stuff," said Leroy.

"Gee," said Stuart, "Sandra Hollins? She's in my homeroom. Did you take her out, Leroy?"

"Yeah, I take her out once in a while."

"Does *she* go all the way?"

"Don't ask me, liver lips. Ask Gray. Or find out for yourself, if you know how." The bloom was off his day. He resented that his reputation was his only distinction, the only reason they suffered him. It irritated him that Stuart should prefer his testimony to Gray's, for it proclaimed what they all knew; that, in this respect, as in so many others, he was not of their fraternity. Theirs were still the bonds of chastity, despite their talk, which Leroy suspected to be just that. Though they lapped up everything he told them, in their hearts they were offended. And even he had come to realize that his experience was a mark not of his skill but rather of his class. They had been sheltered. No one had bothered in his case. But they would soon catch up with him, and then he would hold no novelty for them at all.

That night, the expectations of the minister's daughter were dashed. She had heard so much about him, and things had looked so promising last night, but tonight he walked her straight home from the movies and left her on the porch with a "Be good in church tomorrow."

"Well!" she said to herself as she flounced in. "Who does he think he is?"

John Donnelley, gentleman farmer, was planning his annual harvest picnic. October, Indian summer, one hundred and fifty of the county's finest families, forty barrels of apple cider, one hundred pumpkin pies, a dozen cases of

Scotch whisky, and every woman bring a casserole. Horseshoes, tug o'war, rodeo, square dancing, and hayrides. Postponed for one week in the event of rain. He sat down with his wife Grace one evening in early October to review the guest list. It was substantially the same year after year. A few names were omitted, a few added. This year among those added was George Pottsworth, bachelor, and owner of the small South County Feed & Grain Company. "Who's George Pottsworth, for heaven's sake?" asked Grace.

"Feed man. He supplied me when Harvey's shut down because of the flood last March."

"What a memory."

"Public relations, not memory."

When he addressed the mimeographed postcards informing his friends of the date of the picnic, he remembered to add to George Pottsworth's, in his own handwriting, a hearty postscript—"And bring along a lady-friend, George, old man."

The Bollingers were on John Donnelley's permanent list. Not just the permanent picnic list, but his permanent list for all the events throughout the year: picnic, weddings, christenings, funerals, New Year's afternoon, St. Patrick's Ball, the works. He had known Margaret Reed Bollinger since before she was born. He had diapered her, rocked her to sleep, given her a bottle. In fact, as he was fond of telling his friends in front of her, she had peed on him more than once.

In the afternoon of the day John Donnelley added George Pottsworth to his picnic list, Margaret Bollinger received Leroy Baker on the occasion of his second French lesson. She had toyed all morning with the idea of putting it off. He was a dull, awkward, insolent baby, breaking up her afternoon, making a nuisance of himself. However, the fact remained that if she put him off today there was always next Wednesday. By noon she had recalled a dream of the previous night and had decided that the dream was the cause of her reluctance to see him. Although she could not call up his face, had not been able to all week, in her dream a perfect image of it had been reproduced. It was a bold, critical, appraising face, taking her in, noting her deficiencies, comparing her, estimating her, rating her. It was a speculating face; it asked questions and it answered them. He had her down, had her categorized before she even realized he was doing it.

In her dream, he looked at her, sphinxlike and insolent. "Why are you looking at me?" she asked him. He laughed. He came upon her on a white sand beach. He gave her a once-over. "Not a bad bathing suit," he said. She quivered. "Thank you," she said softly. (She blushed to think of it in daylight.) "Don't mention it," said he. He appeared in front of her on the porch where she sat with John. He laughed silently at John, waved to her enigmatically, and disappeared. John, behind his paper, never noticed. She had waked sweating; John slept on, peaceful as a lamb. She slept again and when she reawoke remembered nothing of the dream. She knew only that it would be a bore to have him cluttering up her house that afternoon. But a split-second glimpse of herself in a long mirror, a blur of legs, a white V of throat, a swirl of hair framing a startled face, brought back the dream. She did not stop but hurried on to the kitchen to check Mrs. Haskell's shopping list. When Mrs. Haskell rolled off in the car with the gardener to do the shopping, she poured out a cup of coffee and sat down at the kitchen table. She sipped the coffee thoughtfully, wondering if there were something wrong with her. She lit a cigarette. "Why should I dream about a local high-school boy who probably thinks I'm old enough to be his mother?" The coffee was hot and bitter; she added a little cold water from the faucet to it. "I ought to have my head examined. Wouldn't John laugh?"

She put the thoughts away and turned her attention to the hill at the back of the house. Late zinnias and chrysanthemums, gold and orange and white, fought with the coral asters. A welter of dark grapes bruised the arbor, which cast a black shadow over the filled-in pool. The day was warm. The chirp of a lone cricket remained of the summer cacophony. Leaves, already fallen from the crabapples and the oaks, were gathered in neat mounds over the lawns, ready to be burned by the gardener in the next morning's dew. Enough leaves had fallen already to permit a glimmer of the pale fluorescent guard rail along the wood road to show through the trees. She had wondered lately about the wood road. Sometimes at night she thought she heard a car stop, voices, occasionally the slam of a door, or a horn, as if an inadvertent elbow had brushed against it. She suspected it to be a lovers' lane but John had disagreed. "It's unlikely. They usually go further up the mountain. Voices carry up from the highway on a clear night. That's probably what you hear." But she had her own ideas. She had gone up once, a year ago, to investigate and had found car tracks in the gravel at the side of the road and a pink plastic comb.

She set her cup in the sink. When Mrs. Haskell returned an hour later, she found her, not playing the piano as was customary at eleven in the morning, but, rather, deep in photographs on the upstairs porch. Margaret nodded absently at the woman, who made a sour quirk at the corner of her mouth and vanished down the stairs. Mrs. Haskell disapproved. "It's livin' in the past like that gives her them big black eyes. The future may not look as bright when you're gettin' on as you remember the past was, but it's a lot closer if you only knew it." Mrs. Burdick concurred.

The photographs were not in order. In fact, they could not have been in greater disorder. She rummaged furiously through the box discarding the ones she did not want to look at, making a small pile of the ones she did. The box emptied, she dumped the larger pile back into it, scooped up the others and moved to a table in a sunny corner of the porch. She studied the photographs carefully, even avidly. She held her life, her thirty-two years, in her lap. The snapshots of her family, of her childhood, did not hold her interest. Several slipped off her knee onto the floor. She bent to see which they were, pounced on one and sent the rest skittering across the floor. It was the one in particular that had been in her mind all morning: the only one ever taken of herself with Teddy. It had been taken at the edge of the Donnelley pool. He, in his white swimming trunks, sat on the edge of the diving board, his thin muscular legs dangling. She stood beside him, as if to protect him almost, straight and awkward, yet with the silent arrogance in her eyes, her frown, her faint smile, of a young girl in love for the first time.

She picked up a magnifying glass to inspect herself more closely. Her face, although thinner, seemed softer then than now. Her figure had improved. "Was my hair really that light? I was seventeen, Leroy's age. I was a hot ticket in those days. That's what Teddy called me." She tucked the photograph in her pocket, and left the others on the floor for Mrs. Haskell to attend to. "What a God-awful name: Leroy!" She bounded down the hall to her room. "Why doesn't he call himself Roy, or Ralph?"

Little did she guess how fond Leroy was of his name. Ever since he had first studied French, three years before, he had doted on it. Le-roy. Le roi. The King. "R. LeRoy Baker," he planned to sign himself someday. Someday, when he sat behind a big shiny desk in an office in New York City and dictated letters to girls in tight dresses.

R. LeRoy Baker, at the moment, however, was pressed to solve an algebraic equation. He sighed and rolled his eyes in exasperation (an expression learned unconsciously from his mother) toward the ceiling, letting them, on the downstroke, flicker ever so deftly over Stuart's paper. He gnawed at his pencil, as if deep in an algebraic convolution, looked up thoughtfully, noted the teacher's lowered head, glanced again at Stuart's paper, and solved the equation. The bell rang. He passed his work to the front of the room and strolled to the door where a little girl in a tight sweater waited for him, the minister's daughter. He clapped his hand on the nape of her neck and propelled her down the milling corridor toward study hall. "Rough day," he said. "Wait'll you're a senior." She bobbed trustingly along beside him, smiling to have caught such a fine young man.

He declined her generous invitation to walk her home after school ("my mother's day at Red Cross," she murmured slyly), and spent the study period planning his strategy for the second lesson with Margaret. He had put away his nighttime fantasies; in fact, the closer he came to seeing her again, the more impossible it became to allow a little daylight on them. "Now, take it easy," he cautioned himself as he climbed her driveway. "Take it easy, or she'll slap you down again." But he couldn't let her walk all over him, either. She had to respect him. That was important too. "If she's not ready at exactly four o'clock," he promised himself, "I'm leaving."

When he arrived, he feared for a moment that he might have to keep his promise. Mrs. Haskell peered at him through the screened door, then vanished into the depths of the house. "I'll count to sixty," he said to himself. When he had reached two hundred and ten, Margaret appeared behind him on the porch steps, out of breath, with an armload of asters.

"I thought I saw somebody coming up the drive. Let me put these in water." She wore a blue sweater with wonderful effect.

In the hall she ran into Mrs. Haskell (who, relishing the prospect of informing Leroy that Margaret was nowhere to be found, was disappointed to see her) and handed her the asters. "Bring us some tea, later, please."

Leroy waited for her on the porch. "Shall we have the lesson out here? The view is so good."

"I prefer to go inside," he said, in what seemed to him a very loud voice.

"What? Inside?" "He has such a tiny voice," she thought.

He nodded. He was not going to be dished out of it. He hadn't come to see the frigging view; it was the house he was interested in. She shrugged and opened the front door for him. He moved across the porch. "What an odd boy," she thought. "Is he going to faint again?" She watched him carefully as he floated toward her.

"Après vous," he said suddenly, taking the door from her. She was startled. He stood very close to her, waiting for her to pass through the door. He was so close that she could see the tiny striations on his lips. His skin was good. Suddenly, he bowed, a sweeping, cavalier bow, well-practiced in front of his mirror on River Street. She laughed and crossed the threshold. "That suits you," she thought. "You'd make a perfect doorman, at some second-rate hotel."

She was annoyed at him for the bow and conducted the lesson coldly, not allowing her personality to show through the personality of Mrs. Bollinger, tutor. She criticized his accent, corrected him rudely, and said *"Mon Dieu,"* when he confused *quitter* with *laisser*. The dark blush on his face all hour finally softened her. *"Ça va,"* she said at half-past five. *"Nous aurons du thé."*

She poured the tea and regretted having cowed him. His eyes were averted and his cheeks still flushed. "He's only a baby," she thought. "He's not Teddy."

"Are you athletic?" she asked brightly, then thought it sounded wrong.

He rested his head gently on the back of the couch, slipped his hands into his pockets and with a thrust of his pelvis, shifted his weight onto the base of his spine. "I'm all right." He smiled faintly through half-closed eyelids. "My coordination's pretty good."

His impertinence dampened her good intentions, and the lesson ended more abruptly than he had planned. After he had gone, she returned to the room and sank onto the couch where he had sat. Daylight was fading rapidly. A cricket, inside for the winter, chirped tentatively from the kindling box. She rested her head on the back of the couch, as he had done, and wondered about him. "Is there anything worthwhile in him," she wondered, "or is he after all just a vulgar village boy?" She plucked at a loose thread in the arm of the couch. "Am I mistaken or *does* he insinuate. *Is* he subtle? Or am I imagining things? But how nice it is to watch him," she thought, "sitting there on a flowered couch, woodsmoke swirling slowly round the house and the smell of it seeping into the room. And he, bent over a French text, pursing his mouth for the *eu*.

"What a huge space he has between his thumb and his first finger. And how shy he is when he first arrives, floating, smiling, stiff, his eyes absent and glazed a bit, pale. There's nothing to it, of course. He can't be expected not to look at someone's bosom if it's there in front of him." She wondered if he had a girl friend, a little pony-tailed girl with C-width shoes and a transistor in a white plastic case.

The beam of headlights swung round the room. She crushed out a cigarette and opened the French doors to air out the room. It was cool for October. She stood for a moment in the doorway. The darkness was pungent with burning leaves and chrysanthemums, but the rustle of a small animal in the ivy on the hillside made her shudder. She locked the door securely and went to meet John.

"Frosty out tonight; we could use a fire," he said as he came in. He kissed her and went to hang up his coat.

The mail girl at the South County Feed & Grain Company sorted out the morning's offering. Most of it went to the accounting department, that was Ed Davies, and the rest, circulars, requisitions, and complaints, to Mr. Pottsworth. There was a postcard this morning too, which she read with interest. The mail was usually so dull. It was an invitation to a picnic.

She put Mr. Pottsworth's mail on Mrs. Baker's desk, sighed wearily, and went back downstairs to type a few bills and wait for the afternoon delivery.

Mrs. Baker picked up her ivory paper knife (plastic but you could hardly tell) and began to slit the envelopes. Mr. Pottsworth waited eagerly in his office for her to bring it to him. It had been a great disappointment to him when, two years before, she had suddenly taken over the function of mail-opener. She must have gotten the idea from a movie or a novel about secretaries in New York City. He could never figure it out. It had always been one of the best parts of the day to hear the mail being plopped into his wire basket. He would often spend as long as an hour going through it. He would read all the circulars carefully, seriously, and then file them away in a folder marked "For Future Reference." But Mrs. Baker barely glanced at the circulars; she just dropped them right into the wastebasket.

She read everything first, of course. That was understood. She brought it in to him this morning. There were five or six letters, unfolded and clipped together. "There's a postcard there," she pointed out to him before she left.

He turned the card over and blushed when he read it. "That's quite an honor," he murmured. "That's a fine family, those Donnelleys." He swiveled round in his chair, turning his back on his desk and on Mrs. Baker, who waited expectantly in the outside office for his reaction to the card. Through the windows he could look down on his empire. Burlap sacks of meal lay piled on the racks inside the shed. Each sack was embellished with the words, in red, "South County Feed & Grain Co." The shed doors, when closed, bore the same inscription, as did the three red trucks that stood in the Tarvia parking area. He reread the postscript: "And bring along a lady-friend, George, old man." He smiled. Who? "Might as well," he thought. She looked especially fetching this morning in a purple cardigan, her tribute to autumn.

"Well, Mrs. Baker," he said, approaching her desk. She looked up from her novel, trying not to appear too interested. "What's the matter?" she asked.

He handed her the postcard. "Will you do me the honor?" He pointed to the inked postscript of Mr. Donnelley.

"Well!" She was flustered. "Don't mind if I do!" She adjusted the cuffs of her cardigan and patted her bob in the back. "High society, isn't it?"

He grinned happily. "Just neighborly."

He disappeared into his office and Mrs. Baker turned to the card, reading it over and over again. She rose suddenly and sailed majestically into his office after him. "Will it be all right if Leroy comes too?"

He was startled. "Well, I don't see why not," he said dubiously. "There'll be so many people there. . . ."

R. Leroy had two more French lessons with Margaret before the Saturday of the Donnelley picnic. Each week his assurance grew. Each week he became more familiar with the house. He no longer walked with trepidation across the polished floors. He put his feet down firmly. "I'd rather live up on the hill any day than down here by the river," he told his friends blithely. "The view is terrific."

At the lessons he found her cool and impersonal; yet he often looked up from his text to find her scrutinizing him with, so he thought, somewhat more than tutorial interest. He had ceased to bait her when he realized that this only aroused her hostility. He treated her instead with an exceedingly polite indifference, which he might have been able to sustain, had he known the disconcerting effect it had on her.

He was not able to, however, for his curiosity to know if she would be at the Donnelley picnic got the better of him. The idea of the picnic had inflamed his imagination from the very start. The invitation, even though so circuitously extended, had catapulted him, in his opinion, into another social class. None of his friends, neither Jonathan, Stuart, Christopher, Gray, Ted, nor Cornelius, nor any of their families had been invited.

"That's because they're new," said his mother. "Their money's new and they're new."

"Isn't new better than none?"

"I wouldn't say we have none, if that's to what you're referring to," she answered finely. "At least what we've got was got honorably. And honor is next to virtue."

Whether this was so or not did not overly concern Leroy. Would she be there at the picnic? Should he speak to her if she were? The idea of seeing her, for the first time, in a social context tantalized him. He imagined himself approaching her, confounding her with his presence, escorting her down a woodland path, engaging her in a soulful repartee, slipping an arm around her waist, assisting her across a rushing brook. His imagination swirled onward to the titillating climax of this scene. He saw himself guiding her, devastated and subordinate, back down the path; he smiled at the tenderness with which she clung to him on the bank of the brook, at her reluctance to part, even temporarily. Oh, it could be a good day. He thumped his thigh enthusiastically.

But what if she weren't there? His heart sank at the possibility. Without her, the day held no allure.

By the next afternoon he had made up his mind to ask her. He climbed the hill to her house for his lesson, stopping once to look at the river. It lay unfolded a mile below him. God's blue and swift it curled around the flaming autumn hills. The bridge, white now against the blue, presented a foreshortened S, distorted by his perspective. It struck him as a good day for late catfish.

At the same moment, Margaret, from the porch where she waited for him, was overcome by the majesty of the same scene. The bridge, its elongated S leaping gracefully from her shore to the other shore, shone white between the blue of the sky and the blue of the water. The afternoon sun tipped over the hill, setting a stupendous conflagration. Woodsmoke and chrysanthemums assaulted her. Her senses, alert to every nuance in the familiar scene, cried out with the beauty of it. With a mixture of melancholy, anguish, unworthiness, and a fierce longing to live out some unacknowledged desire, she lifted her arms and her face to the immaculate sky. "O world, O world I love," she murmured.

As Leroy approached the bend in the road below the house, he could have sworn he caught a glimpse of her in the attitude, rather comical, of a worshiping angel at a nativity tableau. "What's up with her?" he thought. But when he rounded the bend, there was no one in sight.

A moment later she answered the doorbell. "Oh, come in," she said breezily. "I'd forgotten this was Wednesday."

He followed the subtle mesmerizing sway of her hips through the rooms. His voice when he spoke was dreamy. "Had you?" He ran a finger, in passing, down the length of a table runner, disarranging the silk tassels. She was lying, he knew; he *had* seen her on the porch. He knew too that her adoration had, in some subtle way, been for him. It was the encouragement he needed.

"Autumn's in full swing. The weeks fly, don't they?"

"Yes, October's almost over," he said.

She entered the stone room where they always had the lesson and sat on the small flowered sofa, instead of in her usual wing chair.

"Assieds-toi là-bas."

He recognized the familiar form of the verb before he recognized the verb itself. He smiled softly as he turned to see where she had pointed. He saw that she meant for him to sit opposite her in the wing chair. She had reversed their positions.

He sat, smiled at her quizzically, and reached, uninvited, for her pack of cigarettes, which lay on the table between them. "How have you been?"

She had not meant to *tutoyer* him and now cursed silently for bringing upon herself his insolent familiarity. "Well. Thank you." She waited coldly as he lit a cigarette. His curiously mobile fingers fanning around the match fascinated her, despite herself, and she found herself almost forgetting her annoyance at him for having caught her on the porch, as his intimacy told her he had done. "Did you do the reading?" she inquired, still coolly.

He began to see that she was not playing games. *"Absolument toute,"* he said.

"Tout."

He sighed. *"Tout."* She was a temperamental one.

They took turns reading. As she read he observed her legs

through his lowered lashes. The sound of her own voice reading the rhythmic passage and her pride in how well she read it soothed her, and her hostility waned. When he became aware of her absorption he let his gaze wander from her legs through the French doors and up through the trees on the hill behind the house. Something white showing through the trees caught his eye. Guard rails. He squinted up the hill, then smiled to himself. He recognized it as the road where he had parked so often with Joanna. He hadn't known it was so close to the house.

"What are you smiling about?"

"Oh." He returned to the present. "I just noticed that road up there. I didn't realize it was so close."

"It's not terribly close. Five hundred yards."

He thought of all the times he had been up there and had never noticed the house. "All those trees must hide the house."

"Have you been up there?"

He looked at her. She wasn't so dumb. "Once or twice. Long time ago."

"With your father, you mean?"

"Yes. There's a great view of the bridge from up there. . . . I suppose." He had put his foot in it. The bridge had not been there a "long time ago."

"There is, yes." She cringed for his lie. "It's your turn to read." And it was her turn to watch him as he read, to watch the boy's flush from the man's feint subside. "But you're wonderful to look at just the same," she said in her mind.

At six o'clock she rose. "That's all for this week."

His heart tripped. If he didn't ask her now it would be too late.

"Maybe not," he said faintly.

She turned back. "Hmm?"

"I said maybe not all for this week."

She cocked her head. "Now what?" she thought.

"The reason I say that is that we may meet again before next Wednesday." He was breathless.

She shifted her weight uneasily. "Yes?"

"Saturday."

"Saturday?"

"I've been invited to the Donnelley farm for the annual picnic and if you're going, then we might see each other again before next Wednesday. That's what I meant by maybe not; maybe not all for this week."

"Oh, I see. Well, as a matter of fact, I think we *are* going if the weather holds." She moved away. "It rained last year, remember?"

"I wasn't there last year."

"Oh. Well, it did. I *think* it was last year." She held the door open for him. "Read the next three chapters."

"Yes, I will."

"Good night. See you next week."

"Saturday," he said firmly.

"Oh, of course!"

"Good night."

"Good night, Leroy." She stood at the door and watched him disappear down the drive. As he turned onto the road she saw him flick his collar up, tuck his French book under one arm and jam his freed hands in his pockets. There was a jauntiness to his step. Somehow, she felt, he had got the better of her in some obscure way. Suddenly, the thought occurred to her of the hearts he would one day break. She turned from the door into the silence of the house.

❋ CHAPTER FIVE ❋

To Margaret, the Donnelley picnic now presented certain unanticipated possibilities and she spent the evening planning what she would wear and how she would look and what she would say to him when they met.

She found the idea of him seeing her socially—seeing her among her contemporaries—exciting, precisely because her "contemporaries" were all older than she; they were mainly John's friends and his age, forty or more. Compared to those women, she seemed a mere girl. She had some deep egotistical desire for him to see her as a woman having fun at a party, to dazzle him with her public personality. She wanted him to stop thinking of her, if indeed that *was* how he thought of her, as a middle-aged housewife with too much money and too much time on her hands. After all, she was young enough to have danced to "Rock Around the Clock" by Bill Haley and the Comets. She remembered *that* well enough. She had been twenty-three, John thirty-three, and it was the summer of 1955, the summer he was pressing her to marry him. He had watched her from the sidelines as she danced to the first rock record known to man, having the time of her life. And afterward he had been so depressed. "I'm too old for you, Margaret. I could never dance like that."

"Poppycock. It's easy." But he couldn't anyway, even though he tried once or twice.

"I was only fifteen when you were born, Leroy, Don't forget that. I'm *not* old enough to be your mother, if that's what you think." The thing was, she didn't know what he thought. He was inscrutable, one moment asking for help with an irregular verb, the next shooting her a look straight out of Paul Newman. It made her want to laugh sometimes. But that was another thing. You didn't laugh at Leroy. She suspected he could turn on you for less.

She left John behind his newspaper and went up to her bedroom. She sat at her dressing table and studied herself in the mirror. Her small, pale face seemed all dark eyes and a pair of tiny dark nostrils. Her hair, longer now after the summer, set off her face in a bell-like frame. She lit a cigarette and watched herself through the fog she exhaled. She looked young and tough and sexy. She slipped out of her dress and into a pair of tight, red stretch slacks, bought the summer before and never worn. They revealed the perfection of her flanks, buttocks, and stomach.

When Leroy saw her in them on Saturday, it was this perfection he noticed first. She wore sandals, a blue turtleneck sweater, and sunglasses. He took her in from her flanks to her slim feet and back up her straight slender body to the soft hunch of her hair. She looked better than most of the dogs he took out. He wished she would see him, call him over, introduce him, show the others that she liked him. In the group of men she stood with, he recognized her husband, her husband's cousin, Ed Bollinger, and Donnelley, whom he had met at the gate on the way in. The fourth was a stranger to him.

He wondered if her husband bored her. Her life must be dullsville with him, he thought, though she seemed happy enough. She could be a real pain in "class," but she had potential. In those slacks. "In some ways," he thought, "we're two of a kind. She eyeballs me like she knows it, too."

As he watched, she threw back her head and laughed, turning slightly toward him as she did, but he could not tell if she had seen him or not because of the sunglasses. She had. She had noticed him when he first came around the corner of the house. She had seen him spot her and now, as she laughed, she turned toward him, protected by her dark glasses, to see if he had stopped to observe her. Satisfied, she turned her back on him and slipped an arm around her husband and up under his sweater. Leroy saw his quick pleasure at this, his reciprocal hug, and their brief kiss. He flushed and turned away, vowing to speak to her at the first chance. He wandered about the grounds, which milled with the county's finest, all of them unfamiliar to him. He recognized a girl from the high school, a pale girl who played the cornet in the school band and who always walked through the corridors alone. She was in the honor society. He envied her now as she stood chatting with a group of adults, at home in her world and quite certain of her right to be there. Although he would never have dreamed of speaking to her in school, he would dearly have loved to be able to join her now.

He had heard they were all Liberal Democrats. They sent their children to ceramic classes on Saturday morning and to the Unitarian Church on Sunday. The men were professors, editors, writers, lawyers, architects, gentlemen farmers, local merchants and tradesmen. There would be few businessmen, executive types, doctors, engineers, school teachers, or advertising men among those present. The divorce rate among them was low. They drank but they seldom got drunk. Their wives wore longish dirndl skirts and sandals and did their hair in figure-eight knots. They taught the ceramic classes, sketched, made bracelets out of hammered copper, drove Austins, Volkswagens and Country Squire station wagons, and cared less about their figures than about their good cooking. They were always smiling.

He saw George Pottsworth and his mother sitting on a bench together, taking it all in. His mother was in fine fettle. She wore her purple cardigan with a magenta and mauve plaid skirt to contrast and a white blouse with lace down the front. He steered clear of them. They were out and he was out and everybody else was in. It was intolerable to him. He walked self-consciously through the crowds, painfully aware of his aloneness. "Fifteen Years on the Erie Canal" rose above the din of laughter and chatter, but in the extreme tension of his muteness he heard only the insignificance of a jangling bracelet and the shrill shriek of a child off in the meadow. He made his way across the hostile field toward the bar.

"Scotch and soda," he murmured.

"Cherry soda? Coming up."

Mortified, he repeated his order, but the bartender had already turned to dive down into the great red Coke cooler and did not hear him. A woman in a soft sweater appeared at his side and smiled at him in a kind, vague way. He smiled stiffly back through frozen lips.

"Aren't you Dotty's boy?" she asked, peering at him through a thick bang.

"No, I'm nobody's boy," he said stiffly.

"Ho, ho," she laughed. "Lit'ry."

"Cherry soda," roared the bartender. "Here y'are, boy."

He pretended not to hear. The woman smiled encouragingly.

"Didn't you order a cherry soda, son?"

He snatched the bottle from the bartender. "Yes," he said, nearly choking with rage. The woman, whom he had already begun to regard as a friend, had, in that split second, been engaged by someone else, another woman in a soft sweater. He waited, but she did not notice him again as she drifted away with the other woman.

It seemed that nothing could save the day, the event, so bright in anticipation, from turning into a dismal failure for him. He was utterly alone and everyone was leaving him alone, as if they sensed that he had come, uninvited, to gawk. He looked around for Margaret but she was nowhere to be seen. The din suddenly became unbearable to him. The "Turkey in the Straw," guitar, accordion, clapping, laughing, shouting, shuffling, eating, pushing, clinking, shrieking, pressed in on him. His head was heavy with a hot rush of blood. Still grasping the odious cherry soda, he struggled out of the crowd, a little frantic, a little desperate. As he emerged from the crush, he looked up to find Margaret and John watching him. She waved, gayer than he had ever seen her, and beckoned to him. He approached them hesitantly, not sure of his reception.

"Hi," she called. "I didn't know you were here."

He smiled and nodded, thinking what a liar she was.

"This is my husband. You've never met." She looked hard at him. "This is Leroy Baker."

Leroy transferred the cherry soda to his left hand and shook hands with John. "Great to meet you, Leroy," said John heartily. "How's the French coming?" He continued to pump Leroy's arm.

"You'll have to ask *le professeur*." He wondered how old John was. Nearly fifty, he estimated.

"My best pupil," said *le professeur*.

They all laughed at this sally while Leroy wondered uncomfortably how to get rid of the soda bottle. Margaret, who had already noticed it, wondered how but a few days before she could have found this gawky pop-drinking boy so threateningly attractive. Yet, something in his posture, in his attitude as he spoke to John, denied the absolute innocence of uncorruption. She recalled suddenly something she had put out of her mind, his slip about the wood road. She wondered whom he had been there with. She imagined the scene; the two in the front seat, heads together, gazing out over the river, tender inexpert kisses, whisperings, fumblings.

"Do you have a car, Leroy?" she asked loudly, not minding that she was interrupting their conversation. They both stared at her for a second.

"No," he said, wondering why she asked when she knew that he didn't.

They resumed their discussion of McCormack tractors, leaving her out.

Piqued, she frowned and wondered if he were lying. "May I have a cigarette, John?" she asked, determined to assert herself. Leroy caught the edge in her voice. John slapped his pockets and produced the pack. She took one. He offered one to Leroy, who took it and tapped it expertly on the back of his hand. She waited for the match.

"Ed took my matches," said John.

Leroy was ready with his. He held one for her but a gust of wind, or perhaps a sudden rush of carbon dioxide from her nostrils as she bent over his hand, extinguished it. She laughed and he lit another. She touched his hand to steady the flame.

"Thanks." She threw back her head and exhaled mightily. "Well, Leroy," she said brightly, "I forgot to tell you before but we won't be having a lesson next week."

"No?"

She enjoyed his fallen face. "We always go into the city at this time of year so they can clean the house."

He was disappointed. An advantage won today would surely have been lost by the time he saw her again.

"I hope you don't mind missing," she teased. "I'll give you enough before I go to keep you satisfied."

He smiled at her. "Well, in *that* case," he said.

Just then a shout went up from the crowd.

"Fire!"

"Fire!"

"The barn's on fire."

They turned to look. A column of smoke twisted up from the roof of the barn. The crowd surged back as one, murmuring. A few people ran toward the building. Leroy could make out Donnelley and his wife. Someone darted toward the house. Two boys ran out of the barn.

"The well!" someone shouted. "Start the pump on the old well." No one seemed to know where the old well was. Donnelley raised his cane and pointed over the heads of the crowd to a shed nearer to the house than to the barn. Several men ran toward the barn, and emerged leading four wild-eyed cows. A few moments later Leroy saw Donnelley steering the McCormack tractor to safety.

The crowd was scattering as if caught in an unexpected cloudburst. Mothers, suddenly aware of the danger, searched for their children. Cars were being started. People were anxious to get away before the fire trucks arrived. The fire whistle in the town began to wail. Car horns hooted. A table was overturned. A child cried. Smoke poured from the roof now where but a few moments before a graceful sinew of it had appeared. Leroy turned toward Margaret but she and John had disappeared. He saw his mother and George Pottsworth running heavily across the lawns to the car, his mother in the lead.

A flame, the first, broke through the roof.

Half an hour later the barn burned merrily, the flames

fed by the loftful of hay and fanned by the brisk late afternoon breeze. The firemen could do nothing but prevent it from spreading to the surrounding fields of tall, dry grasses, and from there to the woods, the house, the garage.

Half the crowd had disappeared. The other half stood watching the blazing wreck, their faces aglow from the reflection of the flames. Leroy, well back from the fire and from the rest of the crowd, sat himself in a deck chair and watched. It pleased him that the picnic had ended so disastrously. As he had not been a part of their play, so now he did not feel a part of their pain. In his own immutability he sipped thoughtfully from the Scotch he had poured for himself and contemplated the mutability of events.

The setting sun left him in obscurity. No one had noticed him all afternoon and no one noticed him now. Two acorns fell simultaneously with a plop-plop from the oak tree under which he sat. He stretched his legs, crossed them at the ankles, and smiled through half-closed eyes. A dog stood on one of the forsaken picnic tables rummaging in Kit Cohen's shepherd's pie, and in the distance an airplane droned its way across the darkening sky.

Two hours later no one was left at the scene but the firemen, the Donnelleys, their maid, and Leroy. He sat, still undetected, in the darkness in his deck chair and watched as the maid and Mrs. Donnelley cleared away the debris of food and dishes. A spotlight flooded the picnic area, but even it did not include Leroy in its circle. Two men came to fold the rented chairs and stack them in a pickup truck. Another man walked about the field spearing paper cups and plates with a barbed pole. The boy quietly poured some more Scotch into his paper cup but he dared not light a cigarette, although he wanted one, for fear of being discovered.

The barn, now only a smoldering remnant of itself, sizzled angrily from time to time. Only one truck and two sleepy firemen remained to watch its final death. Doors slammed and the pickup truck rolled away down the hill; the cows lowed restively in their unaccustomed shelter, a station wagon was loaded with a dozen sacks of garbage and Donnelley drove off with it to the village dump. He returned in half an hour and paid a last visit to the glowing foundation of the barn. He called good night to the firemen, then went into the hut to tuck in the cows. The garage doors were pulled down, the spotlight extinguished. Lights went on on the second floor of the house. Leroy sat in his chair until all was dark and still. Then he screwed the top on the Scotch bottle, carefully placed it beside the chair, and started a little unsteadily across the field. A dog barked as he neared the house and he could hear the tch-tch-tch of the electric pump.

It was fourteen miles to River Street and he walked the whole way. Sunday dawn was breaking over the water as he stumbled into bed.

At the first sign of smoke, the Bollingers had made their way through the crowd, which swarmed and buzzed now like a hive of smoked-out bees, to the house, where John called the fire department. "Looks like we've got a little work for you up here at the Donnelley place." But by the time he had replaced the receiver the first flame had already begun to lick its way across the roof.

People thundered past the house and down the driveway to the field where their cars were parked. Margaret saw a woman who resembled Ralph Baker's widow thud past the porch.

Donnelley came out onto the porch. "Don't stay, Margaret," he said, "the fields are likely to go up."

"The trucks will be here. John just called."

"They can't do any good for the barn."

The whole roof was ablaze. "I'm glad the crowd is thinning out anyway. Less commotion if it does spread." He turned his back to the fire and sat on the porch railing. "If these damned fools jam up the driveway with their cars, the trucks won't get up the hill at all."

"I heard the Demerest boys say they were going down to direct traffic out the old logging road way," she said.

He nodded. Over his shoulder she scanned the field for Leroy. Several dozen people stood around the barn to watch the progress of the blaze but he was not among them. There was another group farther away, across the fields at the edge of the woods. She took off her glasses, the better to see the red of his sweater. Squinting and shading her eyes against the sun, she tried to pick him out, but there were several red sweaters and none of them seemed to be on him.

"What are you looking for?"

It was John on the ground below the porch. She felt a twinge of annoyance, as if he were to blame for spoiling the picnic, or at least what the picnic was to have been for her.

"Nothing."

"Well, shall we go, then? Or do you want to stay for a while?"

"We might as well go," she said. "There's nothing we can do."

And so they left, but not before she had started out across the field on the pretext of finding her sunglasses (which were tucked in the sleeve of her sweater) in order to get a better look at the group of spectators beyond the picnic tables. He was not there. The sun had already sunk behind the trees and long shadows threw the field toward evening. It was after four o'clock and she shivered as she walked back to her husband. November was upon them.

They started home in a silence that she broke by asking him what he thought of Leroy. His face brightened. "Very nice," he said, as if he were commenting on a new salad dressing. "A very nice boy. Polite, well-mannered, a credit to old Baker. Not one of these crazy Beatle types."

"You really liked him?" Her voice quivered a little with pride.

"Oh, yes. He's a fine boy."

"Well, he comes on straight, but sometimes I get the impression that that's all an act." She found it difficult to say exactly what she meant. "I mean, sometimes I feel he's laughing at me. Didn't you get a feeling that he was pulling the wool over your eyes?"

"No, not at all."

"I don't know," she sighed. "There are times when I just think he's full of baloney."

"I liked him."

"My," she teased, "I'll have to tell him what a conquest he's made."

"You won't be seeing him for a couple of weeks," he reminded her.

"Oh, I forgot." They resumed their silence. If she had felt let down that the picnic had been ruined, she now felt even more depressed at the recollection that she would not be seeing him for two weeks. It was unfair to have sprung that on him. He had not been able to conceal his disappointment. And then to have left, as she so deliberately had, without saying goodbye. . . . Her remorse grew. She must make it up to him.

Lights were flickering on in all the little houses along the way. Children raced homeward along the road on bicycles and on foot across the darkening lawns. An aproned woman appeared on a porch to urge her child on through the twilight; she lifted her face to sniff at the woodsmoke and humus smell that hung in the air, then disappeared from view as the car moved on along the country road. Margaret touched her throat as if to smooth away the thought of the child on whose grave the leaves of six autumns had already fallen. She felt, suddenly, a great tenderness for Leroy, a child himself. And a child that it would be fine to do something for. "Perhaps we could do something for him?"

"Something for . . . ?"

"Leroy."

"Oh. Well, you are, dear, you are."

"Something more, I mean. We have so much. If we could give him a chance, maybe he would amount to something." Her altruism was not indefensible (it would be satisfying to see him get on), but it was not selfless either. It would be nice also to have him around, to see him more often.

"Oh, he will, he will. Do you want to pick up some cider?"

She nodded. He pulled in to a roadside stand. She watched him from the car as he strode to the bleachers and moved among the vegetables, choosing peppers and grapes, apples, a pumpkin, a jug of cider. He deposited these in the back seat.

"I've thought of something we can do, if you want to," he said. He disappeared, and in the few seconds between the slam of the door and the reillumination of the car as he opened the front door on his side and got in beside her, she too had thought of something she could do. He closed the door and they were in darkness again. "Here's an apple." They bit simultaneously into the tart juicy fruit. She waited. He started the car, and moved out onto the white highway. He seemed to have forgotten.

"What can we do? What did you mean?"

He stepped on the gas, as he always did when they passed through the fallen-rock zone beneath the Palisades, and spoke, when he spoke, with his mouth full. "Take him to the opera."

It was something. "Do you mean that you and he will go together?"

"Of course not."

She spoke rhetorically and with the convincing sincerity of a woman about to speak insincerely. "But it's too late to get a third ticket."

"But you and he will use the two we have, naturally."

"Oh." She paused carefully. "Won't you mind missing it?"

His answer was of no interest to her. Her mind raced on to the evening at the opera. She was very pleased. It would make up to him for the picnic.

"Which night?" she asked, laying her plans. "We have tickets for three."

"It doesn't matter." He had already dismissed the subject; for him it was simply an opportunity to avoid the opera. For her, it would be a second chance to see the boy socially, to sit beside him in the atmosphere of intimacy provided by a darkened theater, of supper afterwards, tête-à-tête. Yet, it would be an occasion on which her role could be, if necessary, if he made it necessary, the safe one of instructor, benefactor.

She spent all Sunday thinking of it—of what she would wear, of how she would have her hair done, of what they would say, of the looks that would pass between them. It was a prospect made more delicious by the fact that he would see her, for the first time, in the evening—in her evening clothes, wearing her evening perfume, and an evening smile.

But, there was also the other aspect of it, equally exciting to contemplate; she would be opening a new world for him, a world of glitter and gilt, of mink and librettos, of boxes, tiers, and monocles. She would be exposing him to the *beau monde,* introducing him to the Faust story, to Gounod, to the best. It was what she could "do" for him, and it fired her with an intensity of tenderness toward him to think of it. She would redouble her efforts to improve his French; she would expose him to music, to art; she would direct his reading; lend him her museum pass; guide him gently but firmly toward the college that would best prepare him to demand the best. For Christmas she would give him a subscription to a worthwhile magazine—she had just the one in mind. In short, she would make something of him.

And it was Gounod to start. She ran up the stairs, full of energy and ideas, to write to him. When the note was finished she clipped it to a copy of a *Faust* libretto, souvenir of another season, put it into a manila envelope and left it on the downstairs hall table to be mailed.

Mrs. Haskell, on picking it up the next morning, shook it angrily. "Mr. R. Leroy Baker, is it? Ain't we grand." She turned it over and saw that it was not sealed, only fastened with a metal clip. Since the piano vouched for Margaret's whereabouts Mrs. Haskell felt safe in deftly opening the envelope and examining its contents. She read the note and scowled fiercely. "Ain't we grand. Now it's the opera. Ain't we goin' some." She shook her head.

Later, she said, in relating her discovery to Mrs. Walker, "Ain't it the limit? French lessons not good enough for His Highness. Now it's the oppra."

"What next?" commiserated Mrs. Walker. "Just tell me what next?"

Leroy was beside himself with joy after digesting the information in the manila envelope. At last, at last, he was beginning to get something out of it all. By the end of the day he was fancying himself as somewhat of an opera buff. "I'm going to the opera," he imagined himself saying casually to his friends at school. "I'm going to the opera. *Faust*. Wouldn't miss it for the world." And then, the day after, he could say, if the subject happened to come up, "The opera? Oh, I was at the opera last night. Not a bad show."

He had a firm idea of what the well-dressed man about town wears to the opera: tails, striped trousers, patent-leather slippers, spats, silk top hat, pearl-gray gloves. His wardrobe, however, included none of these items. When he left River Street to board the bus to New York, he was wearing his dark blue suit, a white shirt, a red tie, and a new pair of gold socks. His brown tweed winter overcoat and his trench coat had both been left in the closet on the theory that the former didn't "go" with the rest of his outfit and that the latter was too shabby. When he arrived at the Plaza, where she was staying, his face and hands were pinched and red from the sharp November blasts.

She answered his knock and realized the instant she saw him what a mistake she had made. She, who had spent the better part of the afternoon preparing herself for the occasion, bowled Leroy over with her décolleté, her upswept hair, and her French perfume. She blushed at his admiring whistle and showed him in. His suit, tight across the shoulders and too short in the arms, was appalling. His collar, turned up against the wind and hastily turned down, was still askew in the back. His ears were red with cold, so red they looked as if they'd never be white again. After the first moment, she avoided looking again at his bow tie, the note that he believed lent formality to his costume. But his socks, his gold socks, were the last straw.

"My," she said dully. "You look cold. Is it cold out?"

He blew on his fingers, then shook his hand vigorously as if to start the circulation. "I'll say."

Her mind flew to her closet. "Perhaps I'd better put on something warmer," she said weakly. The odor of his Old Spice was turning her stomach.

"Oh, no," he said loudly and firmly. "Oh, no, don't do

that. That's a great dress. I've never seen such a great dress." He took it off with his eyes as he spoke.

She was stuck with it, she saw, as she was stuck with him. She groaned inwardly as he rested his feet on a brocade hassock, groaned at the socks that danced briefly before her eyes. "Would you like a cup of tea? Or something else?" She watched, fascinated and disgusted, as he tugged an eyelid down to his cheekbone and rolled the other eye hideously. "I've got some soot in my eye," he said. "Could I use the men's room?"

"Of course." She walked self-consciously across the suite to open a door, aware that his eyes dwelt salaciously upon her bare back. "It's down there."

He bowed. *"Merci beaucoup, Madame."*

She fled to her bedroom. There was nothing she could do. Her hair was up and it had to stay up. She kicked off her silver sandals and shoved her feet angrily into a pair of dark pumps. She ripped off her jewelery, extricated the tiara from her hair and flung it all onto the bed. She rummaged through her drawers for a stole to cover up her ill-planned nudity, cursing the boy for his gaucherie and herself for her stupidity.

When she returned to the living room, he was there. She managed a wan smile. They would stay in their seats between the acts, she decided, and no one would see his tie or his socks. A post-opera supper club was obviously out of the question, so she ordered turkey sandwiches from room service. Thus, they almost missed the curtain.

"I've got one of those bubbles in my ear from the wind," he whispered as they entered their seats. "Hope I can hear the show." She flashed him a false smile and settled disdainfully into her seat, thinking of sows' ears and silk purses. He helped her slide her mink coat off her bare shoulders, whereupon she discovered that she had left her stole in the taxi. She cursed to herself and decided to ignore him altogether, although she could not ignore the fond look he cast upon her bosom before turning his eyes stageward.

During the performance she stole a glance at him now and then. He looked better somehow; his hair was smoothed down, his collar in place, his coloring returned to normal. Despite herself, she found his curving cheek, angular half-parted lips, and the brush of his lashes disarming. He breathed softly and once, as if out of a dream, started to look at her, rubbing his cheek in a manner so charming that her heart softened. She forgave him the socks and told herself she was a snob. She returned her attention to the stage and was not aware that she spent the rest of the act leaning ever so gently against his shoulder. She was aware only of the slightest of pressures, so slight that she could not discern if it were conscious or not, of his knee against her own.

At the end of the act, he straightened himself and stretched unobtrusively. "Would you care to go out for a cigarette?" This simple query was couched in a tone so tender and solicitous that it made the blood rush to her head. She felt oddly young and submissive.

"Not unless you do," she whispered.

"No. I'd rather sit here with you."

She nodded mutely.

"It's a great show," he said after a while. "I'm enjoying it."

She nodded again. "It is."

There was another silence during which she could think of nothing to say. "You know," he whispered, "I've discovered something."

"What?" she breathed.

"Well, if you don't mind my saying so," he smiled rakishly, "I've discovered that in French your name is Marguerite."

It was part of Leory's luck that he could utter the most banal of remarks and count on the most devastating of effects. The ordinariness of his observation produced in her, paradoxically, the same intense thrill she would have felt if he, in undressing her, came upon the mole on her left thigh, and paused in his explorations to breathe in her ear, "Darling, I've discovered something."

"My name in French is Le Roi," he continued.

She swallowed and nodded.

He smiled at her, then lost interest in the conversation and leaned forward in his seat to look down upon the bustle in the orchestra. Men in evening clothes assisted women back and forth through the rows from one nucleus of conviviality to another. Arms, bare but for circlets of diamonds, floated languorously in the air in greeting. Margaret took the opportunity to look him over. She saw, despite the ill-fitting jacket, that his back was long and well-shaped. It was a swimmer's back, a back like Teddy's. She imagined the gentle channel that ran the length of his spine. She looked furtively at his profile. Written all over it were the envy and admiration he had for the fashionable scene he watched. A signal warned the audience to reassemble. He studied them in silence as they poured in from the outside corridors. The lights dimmed and he settled back beside her. "I guess I'm not exactly in their class," he said softly, "or yours either, for that matter."

"Don't be ridiculous," she said, flushing.

After the performance they moved slowly from the house with the sparkling, chattering crowd. She nodded to a couple, friends of John's, and saw that Leroy followed them with his eyes down the carpeted stairs. He took her arm, more to feel the mink than to guide her. It was raining and windy outside. "Try to get a taxi," she said.

She stood under the marquee while he made his way

to the street and watched him as he dashed to and fro after the elusive cabs. He lacked the right technique for procuring one, and time after time she saw him elbowed out of the way—done in by a stunning figure in white tie, or a sleek-haired camel hair-coated contemporary. She shivered and drew her coat around her. He looked back at her once and shrugged foolishly as he missed another chance. She nodded. Just then one drove up and she rushed out from under the marquee and opened its door. "Leroy!" she shouted. He shrugged again and came toward her. His face and head glistened with rain; the shoulders of his blue suit were soaked. He followed her into the cab. "Good work," he panted, "I'm new at this game." She smiled frostily, her momentary desire for him thoroughly dispelled.

"And how are you getting back to the country tonight?"

"Bus from the bridge," he said humbly.

She rolled up her side window. "Drive through the park to Seventy-ninth and back down Fifth to the Plaza," she said to the driver. "Then you can take this boy to the terminal at the bridge."

She looked at Leroy to see what effect "this boy" had had. He only smiled. To make up for it, she slipped her coat off her shoulders. "Where are we going?" he asked.

"I want you to see a bit of the city at night."

They entered the Park at 59th Street on the West Side. Through the bare network of branches the mansions along Fifth Avenue were visible in unreal silhouette. "Don't look at me," she said. "Look at New York."

He obeyed her, but he wished she would either let him go so he could get home and out of his wet clothes, or take him back with her to the hotel, if that was what she wanted. He shifted impatiently, out of tune both with her and with the brilliant nighttime metropolis. He stared dully out of the cab window as the dazzle of New York sped past. The lake, mirror of the splendor of Fifth Avenue, twinkled unnoticed, black and gold, at his elbow. The planes of the Park revealed now one perspective, now another, of the West Side skyscrapers, but he cared only for his damp collar and socks, and her perfume. The cab pulled out of the Park and down Fifth Avenue.

"Isn't it marvelous?" he heard her say. "Doesn't it all seem like one big stage set?"

"It's great," he said, shifting again. She looked different in the dark. Her eyes took on a look that seemed to say, "I'm yours if you have the nerve," and to pierce him with a nameless desire. He was restless and ill at ease in their unfamiliar conjunction.

"Pull up at the corner of Fifth and 59th and wait," she said to the driver. Her voice was harsh. "I want to show you something; come on."

"Forget it," he wanted to say. "Just tell me what you want." But he had heard that that was the way with certain women. The preliminaries dragged on for half the night. He clambered out of the cab and followed her. She ran across the sidewalk and darted down the stone steps into the park. It had stopped raining. A strong east wind had blown down the last hundreds of hickory and ash leaves. They lay, wet and shiny, plastered to the sidewalk. She turned at the bottom of the steps and motioned him on. "Come look," she called. "Just look." As he advanced toward her, she had the sensation that he was going to walk right up to her, to force her back against a tree, to press his sexy young body against hers, to open her coat. She closed her eyes, but when she opened them, he was merely standing there, waiting to be shown.

"Look," she said weakly.

Central Park South with all its unapproachable chic, splendid hotels, its lacy, turreted roofs, its fashion-artists' skylights, its indomitable glamour, shimmered above them.

At the corner blazed the Plaza, eternally vigilant. As their eyes became accustomed to the shadows, a silent row of twinkling towers sprang up and flourished against the western sky, far away. He waited and wondered what to do, what she wanted him to do.

"You're beautiful," he said finally.

"Come, come." Teasingly, chidingly, but pleased.

"Is that what you want?" he asked her in his mind. Aloud, he said, "You are."

She turned her head slightly so he could get an improved view of her better profile. She found him exciting, but only as long as he didn't speak. "Do you have a cigarette?"

He lit one and handed it to her. A mallard, disturbed by their voices, fluttered in the reeds and floated sleepily out onto the lake. A gust of east wind swirled a twist of leaves around them. One struck her in the face. "I guess it's time for you to go," she said faintly. "That taxi's still waiting." *"Now,"* she thought, *"I want you."*

"Well, I had a lovely time," he said, shuffling his feet.

"I'm glad." The moment had passed. They reached the top of the steps. She thrust a bill at the driver and turned back to him. "I'm glad you enjoyed it. I'll see you a week from today."

He nodded. She pushed him toward the car. "Good night."

"Thank you very much," he said. "It was lovely. Thank you and good night."

"Good night, Leroy."

"Good night," he said again, "and thank you."

She waved and dashed across the street to the hotel. That night sleep was a long time coming. As she lay waiting for it, she told herself she was a fool. You're supposed to teach him French. Can't you leave it at that? What are you trying to prove? What are you *doing?* She knew that what she was doing was out of character, terribly unlike her, but she couldn't stop herself. She didn't care. He was no longer a boy merely to teach French to; he was the catalyst for releasing in her a possibility that no one else had ever seen, a possibility for . . . for what? She found it hard to identify; perhaps it was a possibility simply for living. He made her want something: life, excitement, action, things she had never really known. He made her want them by looking at her in that way he had, sucking her into a powerful eddy of ideas and desires. She was suddenly sick of her isolation, bored to death with her life.

She heard a police helicopter whirring over the Park and recalled the jet whose speed had broken her window in August. Now it was Leroy who was shattering her windows, the windows she had slammed shut when Anna died. She got out of bed and lifted the shade. Below, the streets were quiet and orderly, the Park a sleeping forest, but somewhere, somewhere in the city people were living. "Make way for Maggie," she said softly to the night. "Here she comes."

❋ CHAPTER SIX ❋

SHE could hardly wait for the week in New York to end so that she could get back to the house and to him. The next lesson would fall on the Wednesday before Thanksgiving.

School was let out at noon that Wednesday and Leroy had four hours to kill before the lesson. He started down the hill toward the village, heading, almost automatically, for a bar and grill off Main Street where the main attraction was the owner's daughter. She was perched on a stool at the bar.

She did not bother to turn around when he pushed open the door. She could see that it was he through the dark blue mirror behind the counter. "Well, look who's here," she said sarcastically. She carefully steered an emery board around her right index finger.

He ignored her and set his books down on the end of the veneered bar. "Hello, Mrs. Babcock," he said elaborately. "You're looking very well today." He always flattered girls' mothers. He found it often had the effect of arousing a sweet young thing to a fine, and rewarding, pitch of jealousy. Mrs. Babcock, who stood at the counter shredding cabbage, smoothed her slacks down over her belly and did a little shimmy.

"Not bad for an old horse," she said.

Leroy looked around. "And where is Mr. Babcock?"

"He went on a three-day bender and now he's sleeping it off, the bum," the woman said. "Want lunch?"

"No, I thought Jo and I might take a little walk," he said.

"Just because you're wearing them tights don't give you the right to sit like that, Miss," said the woman, turning suddenly and savagely upon her daughter. The girl wore a pleated skirt that came six inches short of her knees when she was standing. Now, with her legs arranged in a rather neat right angle, one stretched out along the stools, the other dangling toward the floor, it formed a taut triangle.

"It's a free country," she said, wetting the nail she was working on with her tongue. A cigarette smoldered within arm's reach.

"She needs the back of my hand," said Mrs. Babcock to Leroy.

"Maybe she needs a little exercise," said Leroy sententiously.

"Can we take the car, Ma?"

"No, you cannot take the car."

"Thanks."

"Only because it's Leroy you can take it. You're the only one I trust, Leroy."

"That's very nice of you, Mrs. Babcock," he said. "I hope I live up to your trust in me."

"Oh, you," she said. "You're a fast talker if I ever saw one." But she liked him. He was a cut above the others, that was easy enough to see. And he was a good boy, too. She put on some lipstick after they had left, and a black sweater that made her look thinner.

"Well, where shall we go?" he asked when they were in

the car. She switched on some rock 'n' roll and moved her hips in a bouncy little rhythm, snapping her fingers in time with the music. "Where do we ever go?"

He smiled and turned the car up Main Street.

"Hey, you gotta take me for a ride first," she said.

"I don't *have* all day," he said. "I have a lesson this afternoon."

"What time?"

"Four o'clock."

"So. Four. It's half-past twelve now. You don't have time?"

"O.K., O.K."

"I gotta get back by four anyway," she said, taking out her compact. "I gotta big date tonight."

They drove around the village streets for twenty minutes or so. She knew the words to all the songs and changed the station every time a commercial came on so she could keep up a continuous concert.

"Why don't you leave it alone," he said finally. "You're bugging me with all that switching."

"Well, you're bugging me." She changed the station again. "I don't like the way you look today."

He headed for the mountain. "I thought you were planning to drive around all day," she said.

He found a little fire trail and drove the car in along it until it was hidden from the road. She opened the door and jumped out. "Bring the blanket," she said.

As they wound down around the mountain toward the town Leroy's thoughts were of Margaret. The girl seemed to sense his preoccupation. "Who teaches you French?" she asked.

"Margaret Bollinger. You wouldn't know her."

"I heard of her." She cracked her gum. "How come you wanta take French? Don't you take it in school?"

"I have my reasons," he said. Then he added, "You oughta hear that babe talk French. She jabbers away like a real frog."

"Yeah?"

"Yeah."

They drove on in silence. Then the girl said, "How old is she?"

Leroy grinned. "Old enough to know what it's all about."

The girl snorted. "I bet."

"You wanna bet?"

"You oughta take English lessons instead," she said. "Do you wanta lay a little wager?"

"If it's alive I'll lay it," he said.

"Screw you," the girl said softly.

"You don't believe me. Is that what you're sore about?"

She turned her head away. "You give me a royal pain," she said.

"You don't have to be a genius to figure it out," he said. "Everybody knows these society dames are dying for it."

"So does that mean *she's* dying for you?"

"You're jealous," he crowed.

She turned the radio up to drown him out.

He turned it down again. "Look where I'm taking you." In the dusk the mountain roads all looked the same: black Tarvia, lined with shining black bare-boned trees, with the river, gray and choppy, appearing now and then through a break in the forest. The bridge floated luminously in the haze. It loomed nearer, then disappeared, then returned again, specter-like and far away, only to appear again unexpectedly, like a ship in a fog, at a turn in the road.

"I want you to see where she lives," he said. He turned in to the wood road, careful not to drive too fast lest he send a shower of gravel down into her garden, careful to keep his lights dim lest the beam attract her attention. He stopped at the widening in the road just behind her house. "Down there."

The girl peered out of her window through the dusk. Only the tiled roof could be seen. "I didn't even know there was a house down there," she said. "We've been here before, haven't we?"

"Yeah."

"So," she said, "coming up in the world, aren't you?"

He yawned. "It's only fair," he said. "I have the ability."

"I bet she thinks you're a real jerk," said the girl.

"Are you kidding?" He was enraged. "Listen, you little hick, she's down there right this minute panting for me. She's walking around the house biting her nails she's so hot for me."

"Ha."

"Aah, you dumb broad," he groaned. "You dumb hick. What do *you* know about it? If I wanted to I could have the run of that place. I'm telling you she's nuts about me." He brought his furious face up close to hers and she could see that he meant what he said. "And what's more," he said, "it don't mean a thing to me. I'll show you what it means." He pushed open the car door and scooped up a handful of gravel from the road. "Watch," he said. "This is what it means to me." He threw the pebbles through the air and she heard them land a few seconds later far below on the tiled roof. They rolled merrily down the roof and then there was silence.

"See," he said. "What did I tell you? That's what it means to me." He made an obscene sign and spat upon the ground. She believed him.

He slammed the car door shut and stood outside in silence, loathing the girl for having forced him to say of Margaret what he only half believed and what he had, moreover, resolved to keep to himself. He liked Margaret. She was good to him, and useful. Now Jo would spread the word around that he was nailing her and ruin everything for him.

"Look," he said, finally opening the door. "I'm late already. You take the car back. I'm gonna cut down this way." And before she could object, he had disappeared into the dusk with his school books. She heard him scrambling down the flagstone steps.

Margaret was indeed walking around the house biting her nails. It was after four and already dusk. A fog was beginning to roll in off the river and she had visions of him having been run over by a car. She sprang up at the sound of the doorbell.

"I'm sorry I'm late," he said. "I got tied up with a friend," a remark he would not have made had he known there was lipstick on his collar, mud on his shoes, and bits of dried leaves sticking to his sweater.

"Well," she said, spotting the signs right off, "I'm not running a Y.M.C.A. class, you know. I'd be obliged if you got here on time." She made him pay for it, and when he left he was no longer sorry for what he had told Jo. "Nobody puts Leroy down," he said to himself as he walked home. "Not even Margaret Bollinger."

She slammed the door after him. "What an ungrateful little peasant," she thought. "Why the hell do I waste my time on him?" But she dwelt bitterly on the thought of the girl who had spent the afternoon with him. She roamed restlessly through the house.

On Saturday night, she suggested to John that they take in the village movie. He looked up from his paper in surprise, as if to say "What's come over you?" It was the first time in years that she had suggested Saturday night diversion.

The short was on when they arrived. They stood at the back until their eyes became accustomed to the dark before venturing down the padded aisle. She followed John, searching the theater behind his back for the familiar head. An usherette, jealous of her duty, hovered, disapproving their independence.

"Where does the high-school crowd sit?" Margaret asked her softly, boldly, pacifying her at the same time with the recognition. "We don't want to get too close to them."

The usherette pointed to a section on the right. There was a row or two of bare-kneed girls and in back of them half a dozen boys in football jerseys. As she scanned the group for him, she saw an usher approach and ask a pony-tailed twosome to put their knees down—a request that was immediately the signal for twenty pairs of knees, male and female, to appear on the seat backs. The mass movement was accompanied by a scattering of hisses and hoots. "Well, let's not sit over *there*," Margaret said virtuously, although she was actually longing to get closer to see if he were among them. Several couples with their heads together intrigued her.

They finally found two seats in the sedate middle section, but she was in agony, so sure was she that he was somewhere in the audience. She got up once on the pretext of getting a drink of water and lingered in the lobby for a moment, thinking that stranger things had happened, but no lean, dark-eyed youth padded down the ramp after her.

She sighed and went back to her husband.

When the film was over and the great Skouras chandelier in its gilded and turquoise egg-shaped dome had dispelled both darkness and mood, she scanned the house again for a sight of him but he was not in evidence. They stood and moved slowly up the aisle with the crowd. The high-school set barged out through one of the fire exits. As they turned the corner of the aisle to go down the ramp, she saw him directly in front of her. He had his arm around a girl and as she watched, fascinated, she saw his hand glide down the girl's back and over her buttocks.

"Isn't that Leroy?" asked John.

At the sound of his name the boy whirled around. "W—well," he stammered. "Hi, there."

"Hello, Leroy," boomed John jovially. "Good to see you." He looked appreciatively at the girl.

"Hello," murmured Margaret, but no one heard her.

They walked abreast, all, except John, unwillingly. "This is Joanna Babcock," said Leroy. "Mr. and Mrs. Margaret Bollinger . . . I mean John Bollinger."

John laughed. "Ho, ho, ho—that's a good one." He squeezed Margaret's arm.

She smiled stiffly.

"Pleased to meet you," said Joanna, tucking her gum into a corner of her mouth.

Although Margaret avoided looking at her, she was aware all the same that the girl was observing her with interest. She took John's arm. They pushed forward slowly toward the doors. A rush of cold air greeted them. "Won't you join us for a cup of coffee?" In dismay she heard her husband's invitation.

Leroy had the sense to decline. "I promised I'd get her home early," he said, sober as a judge. The girl smiled brazenly and popped her gum.

"Well, good night then. Be careful."

"You said it," Leroy said. "Good night. Good night, Mrs. Bollinger."

" 'Nigh', 'nigh'," said Joanna.

"Good night." . . .

"Good night," said Margaret loud and clear.

They hurried away from each other. Margaret was glad to pass through the pool of marquee light into the sudden darkness of the street. The night was cold. They walked the few blocks to the car, past the withered privet hedges, in silence.

"Might have some snow," was all John said.

"Well," she burst out, as they drove away and up Main Street. "What did you think?"

"It wasn't bad."

"Not the movie! . . . *Her.*"

"Well, you know how I feel about Elizabeth Taylor."

She disliked him thoroughly for his density. "I'm not talking about the movie, I said," she snapped. "What did you think of that girl Leroy was with?"

"Oh. Joanna. She's pretty cute, don't you think?"

She stared at him. "I thought she was plain tarty looking," she said.

"Wouldn't be a wee bit jealous, would you?"

"You have absolutely no taste," she said. "Anyone could see she was a perfect little tart." She subsided into the corner of the car and rode the rest of the way home in silence.

She lay awake a long time that night. "How can he?" she asked herself over and over. "How can he stoop so low? He's so much better, going so much farther. How can he waste his time with her, when he has me as an example of what he should be looking for?" John's uxoriousness had given her this confidence, but she knew that John's standards and Leroy's were worlds apart and that what Leroy saw in Jo was also what he saw in her and what John would never see. Yes, in some ways, she imagined, Jo and she were sisters under the skin. But Jo took life and wrapped her legs around it, while she put it on a chintz settee and preached French to it.

"You're snoring," she said crossly. "John. You're snoring." She prodded him in the side. He turned over without waking. A conditioned response. Your whole life is a conditioned response, John. A conditioned response to duty. And mine is, too, she added bitterly. I want to live, she said to herself as she drifted off to sleep. I want to start living a little too.

A week before Christmas she went to an oak-paneled men's shop in New York and bought Leroy a spectacularly soft beige sweater. But she didn't have the nerve to give it to him, and it remained on her closet shelf in its proud blue box. She gave him instead a French language record and signed the enclosed card "the Bollingers."

Mrs. Haskell knew what was in the box on the closet shelf and didn't like it much. She knew too the reason for Margaret's new remoteness, her restlessness, her interest in village lore and sociology. She knew why she spent so long getting dressed on Wednesdays, why she had changed her weekly appointment at the hairdresser's from Friday to Tuesday, and why short skirts and an extraordinary jump suit, so clearly not Mainbocher, appeared in the closet. She knew, most fearfully of all, why Margaret slammed out of the house in the afternoons not to go for a walk as she used to, but rather, abnormally, extraordinarily, to jump into the car and back furiously down the driveway, returning an hour or so later, tired and out of sorts.

Where she went on these winter afternoon forays was not for Mrs. Haskell to know. "It's enough she goes," she said to Mrs. Walker. "I don't have to know *where*."

The first stop on Margaret's daily route was the high school. She approached it from the main highway, which ran in front of it, and drove slowly enough to get a good look at the sports field. She never saw him on the field. Then she turned the corner and cruised around the building to the parking lot, which, she had discovered, was where the students congregated after school. Once she was almost certain she had seen him in a car with four or five other boys. Her heart leapt and she was about to follow when a carload of girls swung in front of her, cutting her off. With a great deal of horn-honking and shouting back and forth the two cars disappeared up the hill and out onto the highway. Margaret went home.

After leaving the high school she usually drove down Main Street, risking an accident by trying to get a glimpse of the familiar figure, casual, rakish, graceful. One day she thought she saw him disappearing into Wheeler's, an ice cream parlor that even when John was in high school had been an after-school meeting place. She parked hastily in a no-parking zone and nervously approached the shop. It was jumping with dozens of noisy teenagers. Some stared curiously at her; one made room for her at the counter, in deference, she glumly suspected, to her age; the rest ignored her. She ordered a cup of coffee and dared, finally, to turn around and look for him. She saw him immediately, leaning against the end of the counter. He had his arm around the shoulders of a girl who was not the one she had seen him with at the movies. They were talking to a second boy; all three tugged at straws. She watched enviously, furtively, jealous of his easy smiles, his charming gestures. She sipped the coffee as slowly as possible, expecting every moment for him to turn and look down the counter at her. When he did, she forced her face to register the surprise appropriate to an unexpected meeting. He stared at her for a second, as if trying to place her, then smiled and waved. His friends turned in her direction and said something to him. He turned back to them, grinned, shrugged easily, forgot her. She left, with shame dogging her, only to find a ticket on her car. She stuffed it angrily into the glove compartment and drove out of her way to pass the wretched little house on River Street where he lived.

She tracked him because she had an irresistible urge to know what he did when he left school, who his friends were, where he lived, where they lived, what amused them. The more she saw, though, the more conscious she became of how alien their life was to her, how far from the mainstream she was.

She sat on the bank of a dried-up creek and watched them surging past her on the crest of the wave. It was as if they owned the town, had taken it over, had made the street in front of Wheeler's their territory, carved it out by their sheer numbers, their fantastic egos, their energy and arrogance. It was theirs after school, and it was theirs on Saturday, for even on Saturdays she made countless unnecessary trips into the village to see what was going on, leaving John on his day off all alone in the house. John was not what was happening.

Leroy knew that she trailed him, but he never let on because he was afraid she would stop if she knew that he knew. And he didn't want her to stop; it was softest velvet stroking his ego.

One January day as she drove through the village looking for him, she saw him a block ahead walking with two other boys. Her heart brimming with good will, she pulled up alongside of them. "Can I drop you somewhere?"

They stared at her vacantly for a moment, then Leroy's face brightened. "Oh," he said. "It's you. I didn't recognize you." They walked around the car and got in, Leroy beside her in the front, the other two in the back. "This is Margaret Bollinger," he said boldly when they were settled. "My friends, Stuart Middleton and Joe Delilio."

"Hiya, Meg," said the latter. "Nice meeting you."

"It's Mrs. Bollinger to you," said Leroy, switching on the radio.

Margaret, a little flustered, laughed nervously. "Where can I take you?" she asked brightly.

"To Paradise," she thought she heard one of them say *sotto voce.*

"We're going to Joe's house," said Leroy. "That's at the intersection of 303 and Greenbush Road." It was five miles away.

"Good," she said, "I have to go that way to pick up some eggs." She wondered how they would have gotten there if she hadn't come along. She felt vaguely taken advantage of.

"Well," he said, "you look good enough to eat."

She could hardly believe her ears, but a sudden tension in the air indicated that the two boys had heard it too. "Thank you," she said, as coolly as she could. They drove on in silence out of the village and down the highway toward Joe's house. Her face burned for the public airing of her private mortification. He reckoned he had gone too far. After a while he said, "Well, it won't be long now."

"What won't?" There was apprehension in her voice. She hoped the two in the back could not hear what they were saying. If he made any more remarks like that she would finish him.

"Oh, graduation—all that."

"Yes." She was relieved. She took out a cigarette. "The lighter doesn't work. Do you have a match?"

He produced a lighter. "Don't be mad," he said softly as he leaned toward her to light the cigarette, "I'm sorry."

She shrugged.

Joe's house was a red brick affair with aluminum shutters. One-dimensional plaster-of-paris animals gamboled over the frozen front lawn. The boys in the back clambered out of the car, thanking her profusely for the lift. Leroy lingered for a moment. "I'll see you on Wednesday," he said. She nodded mutely and watched them bound up the cement walk that wound round the house. None of them turned to wave good-bye.

A half-hour later a frown furrowed Leroy's brow as it rested momentarily against a pool cue in the Delilio basement. The source of the frown was not the problem presented by the cue ball but rather an indiscreet remark of the host. "She got a little sore when you said that, didn't she, Leroy?"

The frown was born. "Are you kidding?" Leroy murmured. "She's nuts about me."

"She sure seemed a little sore," said Joe.

"You got the facts confused, Dad," said Leroy. "She was sore because she wasn't getting it today."

The boys looked at him in wonder. "You're kidding, aren't you, Leroy?"

"Would I kid about a thing like that?" The ball dropped neatly into the pocket.

Their round eyes assured him that they did not think he would.

He was unusually meek at the next lesson and tripped over a footstool on the way out. He really was sorry he had done it. Now everyone would be talking about it. Leroy Baker making it with Margaret Bollinger. In his modest way, he had had to tell them to cool it.

And so it went. It was a wordless courtship, an affair without the advantages of an affair. *"Une affaire des grands yeux,"* Margaret termed it cynically, although she did not yet want it to be more than that. No nuance, no advance, no setback in the affair escaped Mrs. Haskell's notice. "It's just like in the movies," she thought, "all that staring, them mooney looks."

The only intrigue was the intrigue of glances and blushes, of innuendo and intimation. The romance was that of a classroom *à deux* beside a conspiring hearth. The justification was the elevation of the boy, that is to say, the subtle inculcation in him of the idea of the sky's being the limit (only barely admitting to herself how he might apply this maxim to herself). The fascination was that witching certainty that the boy who had placed himself, so to speak, at her disposal was not a boy.

He was becoming the most engrossing aspect of her life and he knew it. He had her, so to speak, over a barrel, eating out of his hand. She thought he was the greatest, though he had come close once or twice to turning her off with those remarks of his. He wished she would let her hair down, swing a little. She came on like she'd like to, but so far it was all show.

He took great relish in tantalizing her. He knew he could arouse her with a look, a certain swift and comprehensive look that said, with consummate eloquence, all the words he thought she wanted him to say. He was circumspect, however; he did not go too far. A look, the hint of an unspoken endearment, a tender regard for her comfort, and his coup—staring at her when he thought that she thought that he thought she was unaware of it. The simple fact was that he did not trust her to the point where he could take the liberty of touching her. He knew that, despite her infatuation for him, she had the power and the pride to turn on him with a good slap, or, even worse, an indigestible taunt.

Leroy had taken it upon himself months before to go to the public library in the village and do a little research into his tutor's family background. He had found a book called *First Families of Rockland County,* in which he had read that her father, grandfather, and great-grandfather Reed were all graduates (and later trustees and directors) of a certain highly regarded upstate New York college. There was even, according to the book, a dormitory at the college called Reed

Hall. Since he acquired this information before it was too late to apply for admission, he immediately sent for the appropriate forms.

One day in February as they watched together the late winter sun fading rosily out of the world, Leroy mentioned shyly and with the proper amount of awe, that he hoped to be hearing soon from the college.

She was puzzled. "Why should you be hearing from there?"

"I applied there for admission."

Her face was a study in incredulity and delight. "Why, Leroy! You never told me that."

"It's my greatest ambition," he said softly. "I don't like to talk about it too much . . . in case. . . ." He cast his eyes modestly downward.

"Why, I can hardly believe it. I'm simply delighted." She moved from couch to window seat. "I didn't dream . . ." Her voice trailed off. "I mean, it's the kind of place I didn't think kids were interested in any more."

"Oh," he said, "how could you think that? It's a real fine school."

She was properly chastised. "Of course, but I . . ." She faltered. Somehow, it seemed a little out of character for him. She couldn't quite put her finger on it but she would have thought something less inbred. . . . "Do you realize," she said, "do you realize that the men in my family have gone there for three generations?"

His eyes widened. "No!"

"Yes!"

They stood transfixed, incredulous, joyful at the coincidence.

"There's absolutely no reason on earth why you shouldn't get in there, Leroy," she said confidentially. "Absolutely none. I'll write a letter tonight."

His eyes grew bigger. "*Would you?*"

"But of *course.*"

It was in the bag. He whistled cheerfully all the way home.

She was in seventh heaven. She hadn't suspected his taste had become *that* good in the last six months. When she told John, he was not surprised.

"See," he said. "What did I tell you? Old Leroy is a good man. He'll go places."

"I can't get over it." She could have crowed.

"But how will he ever afford it?" This thought had nagged at her for hours. "How, John?"

"He'll get a scholarship. Don't worry." He rattled his newspaper, a signal she decided to ignore for once.

"It's not that easy. Things are so competitive these days."

"Hmmm?"

"I said there's a lot of competition for scholarships these days."

"Yes," he said vaguely. Union Carbide had gone up two points again. Steel dropped. That was all right. Alcoa was doing nicely.

"John! You *are* becoming so exasperating lately."

He lowered the paper. "Am I?"

"You never listen to a thing I say."

"But, Margaret, I heard every word."

"You did not." She glared at him, hating his indifference to her moods.

"Now, now," he said. He put aside the paper and went to the sideboard to pour them each a brandy. "Now, now," he said again, handing her the tiny glass. "There's no problem. No need to get excited. You can *give* him the money."

"Oh, don't be such a damned fool."

He was astounded. In all the years of their marriage she

had never spoken to him like that. What was getting into her these days?

"Well," he said lamely, "you can lend it to him."

"He has too much pride," she said proudly, to which he had the misfortune to reply, "Don't overestimate him."

She set down her glass so firmly that the brandy joggled out, and went up to bed.

The next morning she was all smiles. "I've had an idea, John."

"Yes?" Cautiously.

"I can set up a scholarship in my father's name!"

"Well, there now," he said, buttering his toast.

"Only boys from this county will be eligible. Complete expenses paid for four years. One boy every four years. Isn't it perfect?"

"Perfect," he said, biting into his toast.

"The point *is* there aren't that many applying every year from around here. Half a dozen at the most, and if *I* recommend one of them, he'll have to get it, see? Especially the first year."

"It's a grand idea, darling."

"And we can deduct it. There's butter on your chin, John. We'll actually *save* money by doing it."

"You're brilliant." And he meant it.

Three nights later her tax lawyer poured himself an extra ounce of Scotch before dinner. It was a damned shrewd move. He wondered why he hadn't thought of it himself.

The trustees of the college congratulated themselves on having such a charitable and generous benefactor. It was damned decent of Charlie Reed's daughter.

A carbon copy of the letter that was sent to her was slipped into the file of Baker, Ralph Leroy. She read the last paragraph with pleasure.

"Although Mr. Baker's academic record does not meet

every requirement for admission, we are more than willing to accept him as a member of the Class of 1969 and to honor your recommendation of him as the first recipient of your most generous gift. We would be obliged, of course, if this information were withheld from him until the normal admission date in May."

Leroy had caught his train, as it were.

CHAPTER SEVEN

THE Greek Orthodox Easter fell on April twenty-fifth. She sat at her desk in the bay window writing away for ballet and concert tickets. Entertaining Marina was getting easier every year. She used to have to plan parties, which meant calling up all sorts of people she hadn't spoken to in a year, hadn't heard from since Christmas cards. And *their* children were invariably still away at school, or had already gone back. Why the schools couldn't coordinate their Easter vacations, she would never know.

A few blocks of ice still flowed, whirling, down the river. Spring came later every year, it seemed. She sealed the envelopes, affixed the stamps, and dropped them on the hall table for Mrs. Haskell.

The tickets took care of four nights. There could be a dinner or two. Movies to fill in. She could go over to watch television at the other Bollingers if there was absolutely nothing. . . . It wasn't the evenings, actually, it was the days that were a problem. She had studying, of course, but she was such an early bird that studying was all out of the way by eleven o'clock. It was the afternoons. They could go into town and shop. A new spring coat would be nice. She'd worn the hounds-tooth one for three years. And there was always the Planetarium and the Doll Museum.

But she was too big for that any more. Margaret frowned. What *was* there for a great gawky girl to do in New York? The Historical Society Museum, the Stock Exchange, a fashion show at one of the department stores? She *was* a problem, no doubt. Of course, she needed hours and hours every week for daydreaming and washing her hair. Hours. But you couldn't rely on it. Sometimes she let her hair go for weeks, Julia said, when she was concerned about natural oils and drying skin. At fifteen. And she could spend hours in the kitchen with Mrs. Haskell talking about God knows what.

Marina bit carefully at the callus on her third finger, her first callus. From where she sat in the French room, she could just see the lake. A brisk wind ruffled it, sending flags of spray over the gray water. The windows of the old school rattled in their sashes. It was a late spring. A pair of nuns burst across the lawns, their skirts whipping about their legs. She could see the large Greek crosses swinging over their chests as they bustled toward the chapel.

She sighed, lifted her heavy mane from one shoulder to the other and turned back to the formation of the pluperfect subjunctive. Her attention soon wavered again, however, and her eye wandered over the eleven heads inclined so assiduously to the exercise. She thought with comfort that this was the last day of the term. She was the only girl in the sophomore class who was traveling this vacation, except for Alexandra whose father had a farm in South Kansas, not nearly so important a trip as hers. She wrote something on a scrap of paper, dropped it and her pencil on the floor and, in picking up the pencil, tossed the paper into the blue serge lap of Helen, her best friend. The note said, "*Will* this day ever end?"

Helen read the note and nodded sympathetically, scribbled something under the impassioned question, and repeated the pencil-dropping procedure. This transaction did not escape the notice of Sister Michaela.

"Marina Calpacas. Please bring that note to me." Her voice sent ten pairs of eyes shooting round toward Marina. Marina, red to the roots of her hair, plucked the note out of her lap and walked with as much dignity as she could muster to the front of the room. Her long hair swung with trepidation from its barrette. The nun read the note. "And what does this mean?" she asked, pointing to Helen's answer. "What does TGIF mean?"

There was dead silence in the room. No one tittered. Marina cast one desperate look at Helen, but Helen's face had suffused and dilated into an unrecognizable and unhelpful blob.

"Answer."

"I think it stands for . . ." Her voice faded to a whisper.

"Speak up."

"I think it stands for 'Thank God it's Friday.' " She blurted it out, reaching simultaneously to recapture the note, the evidence of their transgression.

The nun slipped the note into the recesses of her black widths and stood up. "So," she said coldly. "You take the Lord's name in vain."

Marina quailed.

"Is that right?" boomed the nun.

She nodded mutely, horribly afraid that she might have an unspeakable accident if she didn't sit down at once.

"Take your seat," said the nun in a wickedly quiet voice.

Hurrying to obey her, Marina stumbled over a pile of books that someone had left in the aisle and sent them flying.

"You will *both* see me after school today," she heard Sister Michaela say.

It was an ignominious way for vacation to start.

Margaret sent Mrs. Haskell and the day gardener to New York to meet the train. *She* had gone the year before and it had been an hour and a half late.

The car turned up the driveway at eight o'clock. Margaret went to the front door to greet her niece, who barged in through the back door.

"Anybody home?"

"Why do you insist on using the kitchen door?" They hurried through the rooms toward each other's voices.

"Where *are* you?"

"Hey!" They met and kissed.

"Big girl."

"I'm so *glad* to be here." They stood apart to admire each other.

"Let me take your coat."

The girl unbuttoned all eight buttons with one slash of her hand. "It's my winter coat still."

"I can see that." She handed the coat to Mrs. Haskell. The girl wore a blue wool dress.

"I see you're finally getting a figure," said Margaret.

The girl blushed. "Maggot."

"And do try calling me Margaret this year, won't you? Come and see John." Maggot—the hated, but much-laughed-over baby name Marina had had for her. She was too old for that now.

"Here's Marina, John."

"Well, well, well . . . my favorite niece." They laughed and hugged each other. "Big girl now, I see." They laughed again.

"I'm mighty hungry."

"We're having something light," said Margaret. "You've probably been stuffing yourself all day on the train."

They both watched her as she ate, thinking of the dead child who might have been there. . . . The long hair, dark as a Greek olive, was glossier than ever. "Have you been doing anything to your eyebrows lately?" Margaret demanded.

The girl blushed. "No." She had shaved them half off during the summer, Julia had written. Her eyes were gray, like Margaret's, her teeth small and white, her skin sallow and smooth and Greek. Her nose humped slightly at the bridge ("like Leroy's," Margaret thought) and her mouth was thin and wide. She would be a beautiful woman, "if she doesn't go fat," Margaret always added.

Marina found herself irrevocably unattractive. First of all, and worst of all, she despaired at not looking American. She longed after the bright, fair-skinned girls who went to the public school three blocks away from the Academy. She envied without end an inseparable two whom she often saw on the way to school—one with a short, sleek bob, the other with a set of bouncy blonde curls. She hated the foreign look of her own heavy dark hair which her father would not allow her to cut. "You'll thank me some day."

Whenever she caught sight of the girls, whose names she had discovered were Margie and Pat, bobbing along Northwestern Avenue ahead of her, she hurried to catch up with them so she could eavesdrop on their delicious conversation: of dates and dancing, of pizzas and pajama parties, of cars, boys, curfews, and kisses. They seemed to her to live an exciting, giddy, utterly desirable existence that made her own seem drab and intolerable by comparison. She begged her father to allow her to go to public school. "You can go to a public college," he said. "Vassar."

It was only her annual spring trips to New York that made life bearable. The memories buoyed her, fortified her, for months afterwards; the anticipation exhilarated her for months before. It was in New York, or rather, on the train to New York that she had met one of the three men in her life. His name was Robert and he was going from Chicago to Boston on some important, unidentified business. He was twenty, she had been fourteen, and he'd bought her an ice-cream sandwich somewhere in Ohio and an orange crush in Altoona, Pa. And when the train was pulling into Grand Central, he had helped her with her coat, taken down her suitcases, and—moment of great blushes—had guided her down the aisle and out onto the platform with his hand at the small of her back. The mere recollection of it had been enough to set her atwitter for weeks and weeks afterwards.

And then there had been Ronald, a dashing numismatist from Buffalo who had appeared briefly but crucially in her life at a dinner party of Margaret's the year before Robert—when she was thirteen. He was nineteen and a sophomore at Columbia. He proved to be a devoted dinner partner, although he was somewhat obscure in his references, and had played "Blue Moon" on the piano for her afterwards. She in turn played "Albumblatt" for him and the evening was enthusiastically pronounced a great success; a step-by-step account of it was recorded in her diary. On leaving, Ronald had presented her with an English penny "to remember him by." When she protested such unexpected generosity, he assured her that there were loads of them around Buffalo.

She *had* remembered him—in fact, she was utterly faithful to him for a whole year, with the exception of Roger. Roger, the tallest boy—and therefore the most desirable one—at Ignatius Loyola, was a member of her ballroom dancing class. Their romance flourished for a few weeks but he had dropped out of the class and subsequently jilted her, she learned, for a girl named Lila from Evanston. Nevertheless, during their brief courtship, he had sent her a Valentine signed "Yours, truly." No greater significance had been attributed to the comma before or since. And once, immemorial once, he had come upon her in the cloakroom, seized her by the arms, and planted on her mouth what she immediately recognized as a kiss. She still trembled with primordial intimations of violence and passion when she recalled the moment and the sensation.

The fact that the names of all three of these charmers had begun with *R* also seemed to her immensely significant and she vowed that she would give her heart to no one unless his name commenced with that letter. She made a purchase at Woolworth's of a glass trinket box with an *R* etched on the lid.

Roger's untoward departure disillusioned her about men, and Robert's failure to continue their friendship, despite his having taken her address and having said something about being sure to keep in touch, confirmed her disillusionment.

"Three men have failed me," she wrote in her diary and wept a little.

"What are we going to do while I'm here?" She had succeeded in spearing two peas, one on each end prong of her fork and was pursuing another around her plate. "Forks should have either three prongs or five, don't you think? It's hard to do this with four."

"Don't play with your food."

She resigned the chase and pushed her plate away. "I'm tired, Maggot."

"Poor baby. I'll get a bath ready."

She slept for twelve hours.

On Wednesday Leroy came for his lesson at the usual hour. Marina had been shooed off to the top floor with a box of old photographs of her mother and Margaret. Margaret put on a black sweater with a deep V neck and drew a wavy line in perfume down the V. She looked at herself in the mirror and knew she had never looked sexier. She reeked of it. The pupils of her gray eyes were huge and black and catlike. She hunched a shoulder till it touched the soft ashen helmet of her hair, tilted her head back a little and observed herself through half-closed eyes. She pursed her mouth in a sensuous little moue. She left the mirror and walked downstairs, her hips swaying. She thought with pleasure of him and the good turn she had done him, was doing him. She fancied that in the past six months he had made drastic steps forward under her tutelage, and not only in French. In every way, it seemed to her, he was a more refined Leroy than he had been a half-year before. Although she knew the attraction he had for her was more than philanthropic, she had, nevertheless, nothing but the best of intentions in regard to him. To make love to him, she had decided, was out of the question. He would no doubt be awkward and that would make her seem awkward. It would be an altogether awkward affair and one not to be countenanced. She did not love him, she merely wanted to improve him and whereas he deserved to be improved, he did not deserve her love. Even though the very idea of making love to him made her go weak in the knees, she could not quite see herself doing it. It was, after all, perhaps, still a matter of class. He might turn up in bed with the instincts of a short-order cook, a prospect that made her blanch. He might be a prude about it, or worse still, a clown, or worst of all, a crybaby. It was quite impossible. And when it came right down to it, she didn't, after all, want to so very badly—at least not want to go that far. It was good the way it was and at least no one would ever be able to say she *hadn't* had the best of intentions. It was her pleasure, she told herself, to watch the aesthetic, sensitive side of him grow and develop under her guidance. But it would be divine, she twitched her skirt and did a waltz step across the polished floor, divine to kiss him at least.

She had been feeling so much better lately, full of plans, ideas, just raring to go. And it was Leroy who was responsible. He made her want to sit up and take a big bite out of life. Things were going to change. She was planning a party. She would have it in May, after Marina left. Throw the house open, invite everyone, all their old friends, all those gay people they used to see. She was going to start doing things. She might even buy herself a teeny weeny bikini and get John to take her to the beach this summer.

The stage, their lesson room, was set. Rain dripped comfortably down the windows, and a fire, one of the last they would have, blazed on the hearth. Pussy willows and forsythia in brown earthenware jugs sang out for spring. She plumped up the couch cushions and stationed herself behind a brocade drapery to watch for him.

Meanwhile, up on the top floor, Marina, weary of the photographs, stationed herself in the tiny cupola window to watch for the boy she knew was coming. She had washed her hair earlier and now towelled it dry, dreamily, absently. Sheets of spring rain waved and billowed across the lawns and thunder rumbled far away. The breaking up of winter, her mother always said. She made a turban of the towel and examined her eyebrows in a hand mirror, keeping one ear cocked for the sound of a car in the driveway. Perhaps he wouldn't come, after all, because of the rain. Her eyebrows had grown back quite the same. Her father had said she was d——d lucky.

A car stopped at the foot of the driveway. There were many boys in it. She carefully opened the window an inch to catch their voices. One of them jumped out, turning up his collar against the cold rain. He waved good-bye to the ones in the car, and she thought she heard one of them shout back something that sounded like "give it to her, Leroy." "He must have a present for Margaret," thought Marina. But he was carrying only a book or two. "He's certainly *very* nice looking." She pushed the window open further to get a better look at him. "My, he *is* handsome."

The movement of the window caught his eye. He stopped in his tracks and looked straight up at her. "Who's that chick?" he wondered.

Mortified to have been discovered, Marina ducked. But her towel turban caught on the curtain rod and was knocked askew. Her hair tumbled down. In her extreme anguish, it was his grin that she was to remember afterward. It was his grin, charming, rakish, understanding, that made all the difference. It said, "Don't be mortified, be amused. Look on it as a joke, something we've shared that we can laugh about together later, when we've gotten to know each other better."

She went pink and hot and rushed down to her room where she brushed her hair furiously and wondered if she would ever see him again. A puddle formed under the cupola window, which she had neglected to close.

Margaret, from her lower level, could not see the car that had left Leroy off at the driveway. She saw only his dark head suddenly appear on the horizon. Her heart swelled with tenderness and solicitation for his loyalty in having walked, as she inferred, all the way from the village in the downpour in order to keep their appointment. However, just as she was about to dash off to put the kettle on for his tea, she saw him stop and look up toward the house. An engaging smile spread over his face, a smile of intimacy, complicity. Startled at first that he had been able to see her through the thick curtain, it took her only a split second to realize that his gaze was fixed not on her window but on one above hers. Who was up there? Mrs. Haskell was off at a funeral. There was no one else in the house but Marina. "That slyboots." Margaret was outraged. "That slyboots . . . spying on my friends." She heard footsteps on the attic stairs; two doors slammed almost simultaneously and then the doorbell rang.

"I'll be damned," she said softly.

She let him in. "Drip here. Do you want a pair of slippers?"

"I'm not wet," he said. "I came in a car."

"Oh." She was surprised. "I didn't hear a car."

He was staring at her. Her shoulders and bosom through the soft black sweater had never looked so inviting. Her mouth was painted and full, her eyes dark, sexy, demanding. As she moved toward him to take his coat, he swayed slightly and closed his eyes against the dizziness of her. She laughed in his face and walked off with his coat. He opened his eyes in time to catch the switch of her hips as she disappeared into the closet.

"My God," he thought. "Is she ever asking for it." "You look great today," he said.

"What?" She was searching in a magazine rack for their text and sounded cross.

"I said you look great today," he murmured.

"Well, the farmers need a little rain for a change." She ostentatiously dusted off her knees. "Let's get started," she said. "I'm very busy today."

She was merciless all through the hour. She swore softly in exasperated French when he translated *éloigner* as lengthen and said, "No, no, no," when he pronounced the *h* in *hardiesse*. She noted his red neck and ears with satisfaction and asked him if he were chewing gum or something.

As the clock struck half-past five, she stood abruptly and, looking at her watch, said, "That's all for today. We're going out early this evening." She waited, resolute and observant as a High Church usher as he humbly gathered up his scattered books and notebooks, pencils, cigarettes, and school sweater. She preceded him to the door and opened it.

He lingered, utterly puzzled, utterly anxious to redeem himself. So much depended on her good will.

"I saw somebody up in the attic when I came up the driveway," he blurted.

"*Did* you? I wonder who it could have been."

"It looked like a girl," he said.

"Oh? And did you think that it was I?" There was just the faintest tremor in her voice.

"Oh, no," he said quickly, too quickly. "It seemed like quite a young girl."

"Oh. In that case, it must have been my little niece, here on a visit."

"She certainly has got long hair," he said eagerly. "I've never seen such long hair."

"You haven't lived very long, Leroy," she said, patting his shoulder and pushing him gently out the door.

She did not wait at the door to watch his descent to the road; instead she stood in the hall with an ear cocked for sounds of doors, footsteps, and windows above. Nothing. But the next day Mrs. Haskell reported not only the puddle under the cupola window but also a small hole, the size of the end of your little finger, cut with a pair of nail scissors in the shade of the front hall bathroom. Margaret told her to buy a new shade and to get it up that very afternoon.

They were seven at dinner that night; the other Bollingers and the Donnelleys were there. Marina took the opportunity offered by a short lull in the conversation to ask loudly, "Did your French student come today, Mag?"

Margaret looked up from her quenelles. "Did I tell you he was doing French with me?"

"No," said Marina innocently. "Mrs. Haskell told me."

"Oh." She broke a quenelle in two. "Yes, he was here. Why?"

"I was just thinking that it might be nice if he could come for dinner some night or something while I'm here, since he's my own age and everything and we could speak French together," said Marina in a rush.

The eyes of three Bollingers and two Donnelleys looked at her kindly. The remaining pair of eyes shot wrathfully round the table. "He's two years older than you," the mouth beneath them said, but no one heard.

"That would be ideal," said John. "Just the ticket."

"Yes indeed," said Margaret in a voice not brimming with enthusiasm. "I'll do that tomorrow."

When Leroy came for dinner two nights later, John went out of his way to be nice to him. Margaret ignored him and Marina dropped a new potato in her lap as a result of not being able to take her eyes off him. Her delight knew no bounds when she discovered, quite by accident, that his first name was Ralph. The significant *R*.

After parfaits and coffee the company dispersed, John to read the paper at one end of the living room, Leroy and Marina into the stone plant room and Margaret to perch uncomfortably on one of the Duncan Phyfe couches, the nearest she could get to their voices. She made a pretext of knitting but dropped three stitches and finally cast it aside.

She could barely hear them. Leroy was doing most of the talking and his voice was so low. . . . Marina laughed a great deal, a great deal indeed. He was talking about school, the teams, his hopes for college. Marina exclaimed and admired, and Margaret, to her disgust, heard her ask him if any other boy had earned his varsity letter in his sophomore year.

It was torture for her to listen to his wooing of her niece, to listen to her niece falling in love with him right under her nose. She raged with jealousy and indignation. He was doing it on purpose, to torment her; *that* was perfectly clear at least. He was still furious, no doubt, about Wednesday. She should have known better than to patronize him. It had put his nose out of joint, all right. This was his way of getting back at her.

She rushed upstairs to look at herself in the mirror. It was not, unfortunately, one of her better days. Her eyes were pale and tense and her mouth was drawn. In despair she slashed on lipstick, bold and bright, and rushed back down again. In her absence they had put a record on. How dare they! It was one of John's, one she had even forgotten they had, the 1938 Benny Goodman Carnegie Hall concert. Mahler wasn't good enough, or Mozart. Oh no, they had to put on the wildest one in the house, though he probably thought it was pretty tame. She threw herself on another couch, far across the room from them. Right in the middle of "Minnie the Moocher's Wedding Day," he stopped the record. "Here's an oldie," she heard him say. "Let's play this one. Elvis Presley singing 'Teddy Bear.' He was before your time."

"I remember him," Marina claimed. But she wasn't actually positive she did.

With despair, Margaret realized he was teaching Marina to frug. She heard their feet and saw the girl's gray flannel skirt flick past the door now and then.

What insults! What ungratefulness! To come for dinner and to leave her flat the minute it was over. After she had slaved all day planning and primping. After all the time and help she'd given him all year. Next he'd be teaching her to smoke, or worse. Then what would Julia and Angelos say.

The instant the record ended she got up and surprised them on their knees in front of the record cabinet.

"Well, that was lovely," she crooned. "Would you like a glass of cider before you go, Leroy?"

Leroy got belatedly to his feet. "Well," he said, "we were thinking we might walk downtown for a soda."

Margaret laughed merrily. "I think not," she said. "It's quite late. Perhaps another time." She felt safe in her generosity; there was only one more day before Marina returned to Chicago.

Marina's face fell.

"All right," said Leroy easily. He turned to the girl. "How about a movie tomorrow night?"

She beamed and blossomed. "Oh, I'd love to, thank you," she said, lavishing upon him a vivacious and utterly new kind of smile.

"But tomorrow is your last night, darling. You know we were planning . . ."

"Please, Margaret. We could go to the second show."

She knew when she was beaten. "In *that* case . . ."

When he had gone, Marina whirled back into the living room and threw her arms around her aunt's neck. "Thank you, thank you," she said. "He's the loveliest boy I ever knew."

John smiled at her paternally.

She was not seen all Saturday afternoon. She had requested a needle and a spool of red thread from Mrs. Haskell and disappeared into the bathroom. Mrs. Haskell listened to the water run for an hour. "Enough to take six baths," she grumbled. She disapproved as much as Margaret did of the evening's plans. "His ideas are too big for her," she ventured grimly. Margaret merely shrugged, for once feeling a bond with the woman. "What could I have done?" She called off the dinner planned with John's cousins for that evening. "Her hair will never dry by half-past five."

And they waited. They had their dinner on trays in the television room, Marina looking angelic beneath the pink tower of terry cloth she carried on her head.

"What are you wearing tonight, dear?"

Marina blushed. "A dress," she mumbled into a soda biscuit. "Just my red dress."

"If it needed mending, or letting out, Mrs. Haskell could have done it, you know."

She flushed furiously, mortified at the attention to her person. "It was just a little something," she said into her milk glass. She finished her milk and jumped up, nearly upsetting her tray table into the kindling box. "I have to get ready now," she said breathlessly.

"Well, my dear child, he won't *be* here for two hours." She saw panic flash across the girl's face. "Oh, go ahead, do. Otherwise I suppose the world will come to an end."

The girl fled. "I *do* think she might spend a quarter of an hour with us before she leaves. It *is* her last night," followed her up the stairs.

They waited. The clock chimed seven, then half-past seven. Margaret thought with satisfaction of the red dress Marina would wear, a frightful wool flannel affair with set-in sleeves, a shapeless gored skirt, and buttons from waist to throat. She had a second thought about the buttons but dismissed it. Marina had some sense.

The clock ticked louder than usual and when it gave its ancient whirr, prior to striking eight, she began to be faintly apprehensive, despite herself, lest he should stand the child up. She stirred restlessly and put down her novel. "It's eight, John."

He agreed that it was.

She sighed and walked to the window. Though it was April, a March wind swung over the lawns, discouraging a turn along the porches. She sought her novel again but her eyes saw only the print. On the stroke of quarter-past eight headlights beamed through the room.

He gave off the brisk aroma, always aphrodisiac to her, of the shaving lotion he favored. The odor brought on a wave of nostalgia for that summer of the other lean, dark boy, who had used the same scent. He stepped into the foyer and, as she went forward to pull the door after him, she caught a whiff of his breath, as sweet as summer grass. At the same time, he reached in back of him to pull the door and as he did their hands met simultaneously on the cold brass door knob. His lingered for a split second longer than was necessary and as he withdrew it, it seemed to her that it caressed her own. But, hours later, in trying to reconstruct exactly how it had happened, she could not be certain that it *had.* She knew only that as they stood there in the dim light of the foyer, he scrutinized her face in that long, slow way he had that stirred her to the core and said softly, "Hello, Margaret."

She swallowed hard and her eyes clouded and wavered for a moment at the surprise and sweetness of hearing him, for the first time, call her by her first name.

"Hi, Leroy," she said, equally as softly, and took his arm to lead him to her niece.

As they entered the living room, Marina came down the back stairs and into the room from the entrance opposite them. But it was a new and disconcerting Marina who confronted them. She was wearing the red dress but a very much remodeled red dress. Margaret went slack-jawed at the sight of her. It was the same dress, no doubt about it, but she had managed to convert it somehow into a barely recognizable facsimile of its former self. She had cut out the sleeves, utterly obliterated the collar, transformed the high-buttoned front into a hand-stitched V, shortened the hem so that her knees winked and beckoned well below its perimeter. With the addition of a wide black cinch belt, several strands of white poppit beads and a beehive worthy of Northwestern Avenue, Marina had metamorphosed into the type that some intuition, some deep, still unacknowledged instinct had told her was Leroy's type. It was an altogether amateur job. On closer examination the hem wavered and dipped, and one side of the V neckline was pronouncedly longer than the other. It was clear that the beehive would disintegrate, Medusa-like, before the evening was over. The rouge, inexpertly and unevenly applied, flushed one downy cheek and inflamed the other.

But the over-all effect she achieved was devastating, to say the least. Her entrance was perfectly, though innocently, timed. They had whirled out of the house and into the night before Margaret had a chance to gasp much more than, "Why, Marina!"

She ran to the window to watch them out of sight and her dismay was complete when she saw, as the car lit up when they opened the back door, a couple in the front seat spring gaily apart.

❋ CHAPTER EIGHT ❋

LEROY made it all up to her the next time he saw her by bringing her a single yellow rose, a trite and fatuous maneuver, but one that redeemed him in her eyes.

Their "affair" was at a standstill. They had reached a danger point, and neither of them dared to go beyond it. He still did not trust her, still feared to risk the put down he felt she was so capable of dishing out, while she, on the other hand, conditioned by a lifetime of propriety, could not quite bring herself to say, even to herself, "I want you. What are we waiting for?" She spent hours, literally dozens of hours, pondering the point. She imagined every possible situation, every conceivable obstacle, every cogitable delight. Her fantasies grew increasingly more wild and more complicated, giving her correspondingly more pleasure and more despair, and her time, before so judiciously meted out to piano, gardens, and library, was now squandered on daydreams.

She stalked him; he let her do it. He liked it. He was flattered. It was making him. It put him in the big leagues.

She made her rounds every afternoon, and every afternoon she found him, lounging in front of Wheelers, dashing back and forth on the school tennis courts, out cruising around with his friends in one convertible or another, or simply horsing around on Main Street. She always managed to catch up with him somewhere, though it was the rare day when she found him alone, could speak to him. He traveled in a pack, a touring basketball team, with a guard to cover every forward. Some of these boys she knew because she knew their mothers; others she came to recognize simply by seeing them so often with him. She resented all of them. "Go away," she scolded them in her mind. "Go away and let him be. Let him study his French. Let him read that magazine I gave him a subscription to. Let him think of me. You're not good enough for him."

Leroy looked for her every day, and if by chance he didn't see her he felt let down and cheated. He was constantly glancing over his shoulder for a glimpse of her blue Mustang crawling down Main Street or prowling past the courts on the days when he had tennis practice. When he and the others piled into somebody's car to go for a ride, he always contrived to sit next to the right-side window in the front so she could more easily spot him should they pass, on a village street, or out on the highway, which happened too often to be coincidence.

The word was around that something was going on between them. Even the teachers knew the case bore watching. And when *they* knew, the whole town knew. She began to fear she had been indiscreet, a realization brought home one afternoon, a Thursday, as she scouted past the school. She noticed a group of his friends in the parking lot behind the courts and, as she slowed down to see if he were among them, one of them turned in her direction, then turned back to the group and said something that made them all look up. Then one of them, she never dared guess who, cupped his hands and shouted, "Hiya, teach. He went thataway," and pointed down the hill toward the village.

Afterward, she was always thankful she had had the presence of mind to give them a blank stare and turn off on a side street that clearly did not lead into the village. She drove home, half blind with tears of humiliation.

The incident shook her to the core. She was sickened at the mere recollection of it. The very suggestion that her name, linked with his, was bandied about in the village terrified her. She began to recall other incidents that in her madness she had failed to see for what they were: the frosty nods of two women whom she had encountered in a bookstore a month before and greeted with a gay "hello," a greeting that now, in light of what she knew, of what they must have known, seemed not gay but wanton; the familiar manner of a youthful clerk in the meat store when she had gone in one Saturday to pick up an order, the license Leroy's friends had taken with her, their ribaldry as she passed them on Main Street, a ribaldry she had allowed herself to be flattered by, thinking it meant they regarded her as one of them, a swinger, a member of the "Now generation," a friend of Leroy's. She recalled with a shudder their looks, their whispers, their jocose nudges, their heightened vivacity when she approached, and cursed herself for her vanity in having imagined them to be innocent of her designs.

She quailed at the realization of what she had done, drew back, dropped any ideas she had had of giving a party, of getting back into circulation. For days she cloistered herself, cowering; then on Monday she went to church on an impulse. As she drove over the country roads to a church where she had never been before, she believed she was doing the right thing, the thing that would put it all square again.

It was not the hour set for hearing confessions but as she entered the cool dark building, she saw by the orange light to the right of the apse that someone else, some other sinner, had quailed in the searching light of that May morning and sought relief behind the convenient grille. She genuflected and slipped into a pew to wait her turn, but she did not pray. At last the rustle of the curtain door told her that the early penitent had finished. She did not look up; but the ttap ttap ttap of footsteps across the porch told her that her predecessor was a woman. She stood and hurried into the box, thinking all the while not of her own but of the other woman's transgression.

She knelt again. "Bless me, Father, for I have sinned." She imagined that her unseen confessor sighed.

"When was the last time your confession was heard?"

She hesitated. "Before Christmas two years ago." Her heart sank even as she admitted it. What right had she to be here? She was no Catholic in his eyes.

"Yes?"

"Since than I have not been to Mass . . ." It was a mistake to have come.

"Go on."

"I have lusted for a man." It was the first time she had thought of him as a man, and somehow the designation did not seem accurate. "A boy, rather."

"A boy? Is this boy a Catholic?" It seemed to her an odd reaction. It had never occurred to her to ask him what he was.

"I don't know, Father."

"He's not related to you then?"

"Oh, no!" That's what he had thought. Through the grille, she saw him raise a hand as if to clear his brow. "Go on," he said wearily.

"I have tempted him, Father."

"No more than that?"

"No."

"How often?"

She hesitated. "A lot."

"You are married?"

"Yes, Father. I love my husband." She wanted to get that on the record.

"And you have desired and tempted a young boy. Is that . . . ?"

"Yes, Father." But he did it first, she wanted to say. The first day; he started it then. It all suddenly came clear to her. *He* had tempted her.

"Did you feel you were offending God?"

She hadn't, not until it had backfired anyway, but what was the point of saying no to that question in the confessional? That was the point of the whole thing. "Not at the time, but I feel now that I must have been." Her answer seemed to satisfy him. He rattled his beads gently and went on with the familiar questions.

"And now you are sincerely sorry for what you did?"

"Yes." "But I didn't really do anything," she thought.

"Will you promise God that you will never see the boy again?"

She was startled. "I can't promise that," she said quickly.

"Why not?"

"I tutor him once a week." She couldn't just not ever see him again. That was impossible. Moreover it was uncivilized.

"If you are truly sorry for your sin you will make this promise to God."

She raised her eyes to the ivory crucifix above the grille. *I promise You,* she vowed silently, as if the Son demanded less than the Father, *I promise You that I shall not think of him that way again.* "I promise," she said faintly.

"Will you make an Act of Contrition?"

"O my God," she started, hoping her memory for the

phrases would not fail her. "O my God, I am heartily sorry . . ." As she bowed before him she saw him make the sign of the cross over her. *"Ego te absolvo . . ."*

She finished and raised her head. She could make him out quite distinctly now, an Irishman. "Your penance, my child. Say a rosary every night to our Blessed Mother."

"Yes, Father."

"You may go in peace," he murmured, "I shall pray for you."

As she drove back home the words *Ego te absolvo* rang through her head. It was as easy as that. *Ego te absolvo*. And she felt truly absolved, too, truly clean, truly relieved, and truly finished with Leroy.

She knew he had compromised her. But he never would again. She stayed home again that afternoon, through with him.

He missed her. Where was she?

On Tuesday night she called him. "Leroy?"

"Oh, hi!" He had been expecting some sign from her. "Have you been sick?"

"No. Why?"

"Well, I haven't seen you around."

She laughed, a gay trill. "Oh, heavens, I've been so busy. We're having a party this weekend and there's so much to do." Yes, damn it, she would have a party. He wasn't going to stop her.

"Oh!" She was calling to invite him to it.

"I'm just calling to say I can't see you tomorrow. I'm up to my ears with this party."

"Oh."

"But next Wednesday's O.K. Read the next chapter and I'll see you then."

"What about Thursday? I could cut practice."

"I couldn't, Leroy. I'm just so busy."

"Saturday?" Wasn't she going to invite him to it? He had been invited to the Donnelley's picnic.

"No. It's impossible the day of the party. Really. I'll see you a week from tomorrow. That's the twelfth." She had said "Bye, bye" and hung up before he knew what had hit him.

What had gone wrong? He hadn't thought *she* would turn on him. She must have had wind of the talk about them in town. "But even so," he said to himself, "she shouldn't treat me like that. She shouldn't put Leroy down. Leroy doesn't like to be put down."

He was afraid now. Afraid she might prevent him from getting the scholarship he had applied for. He was on tenterhooks for a week, but on Monday the tenth, the letter he had been expecting was waiting for him when he got home from school. Full tuition and room and board for four years. He crowed. He pranced. His mother joined him, not doubting for a second that his triumph was all due to her initiative and ingenuity.

The next day after tennis practice he got the boys to drive him to her house. "Don't wait for me," he said. "She'll drive me home." He could hardly wait to see her face. Oh, this would reinstate him. He would make his comeback. There were still six weeks of school. Still time for a little action. He adored her. He loved her. She had given him the world. He would stop the talk in town. He knew he could.

But she had learned her lesson. "That's marvelous, Leroy." She had not gotten up when Mrs. Haskell brought him in, nor did she ask him to sit. "I guess you won't be needing me any longer. I was getting bored with Parma anyway."

"But I still have my final to think of."

"Well, that's your problem, not mine."

He reddened.

"Oh, if it means that much to you, you can come once

more," she said impatiently. "Come tomorrow. We'll review some grammar and you can stay for dinner. John will want to congratulate you. We'll celebrate." She stood and tossed a cigarette lighter into the air, clapping her hands together once before she caught it. "Yes, we'll celebrate your scholarship and the end of our little study group." She laughed. She had said the words "our little study group" with a malice that implied "our little 'romance.' " Leroy was mocked. "Come about six. We'll study after dinner." She cocked her head encouragingly. "O.K.?"

"O.K. Thank you."

As he left the house, the same boys who had dropped him off were passing by. They slowed down and opened the car door.

"What's the matter, Leroy? We thought your girl friend was going to drive you home."

"What'd she do, Leroy? Kick you out?"

"Teach sore at you, Leroy baby?"

He got in the back seat. "Lay off," he said.

"Aw, we never believed that story anyway, did we, fellas?"

"No, we never believed it. That was another one Leroy made up."

"You guys still don't know your asses from third base. Do you have to see something to believe it?"

"When *you're* involved with it, we do."

At six o'clock the next afternoon, Leroy climbed her driveway, perspiring a little from the heat. It was very warm for May. She was sitting on the porch, rocking herself back and forth in the glider, one foot under her, one foot pumping.

She was in a good mood, not angry with him. She blamed herself for the whole thing, for the unforeseen and pernicious turn events had taken. She had been a fool. Just the same, she was glad it was over, glad she had got out in time.

"Hi, Leroy."

"Hi."

They had a drink, he a Scotch, she a vermouth, in the last warmth of the May sun and spoke desultorily and companionably of his future. John joined them for a second round and, at seven, they drifted in to dinner, Margaret a little unsteadily, having had a martini on the third round. John went around the table filling the wine glasses.

"Here's to Le Roi." She said. "Onward and upward."

He flushed.

"These objects you see before you, Leroy, are our first course. Pickled walnuts, in case you don't recognize them. A specialty of the house."

He shifted his weight uneasily.

"Another toast," she said. "To Leroy, R. Leroy. Today Nyack. Tomorrow the world." She drained her glass, speared a walnut on her fork and reached across the table to feed it to him, drawing a startled look from John. "Eat. It'll be a long time before you dine so well."

"More wine, John. For my next toast." He poured a little wine in her glass. "More. Fill 'er up. I've got lots of toasts to make tonight."

"I think you've had enough, Margaret, don't you?"

She took the bottle from him and filled her glass. "Sermons and soda water tomorrow, Uncle John. Tonight we drink. This one's to me. Maggie. Long may she live a little."

Mrs. Haskell rolled a cart in and started serving the main course. "Lobster tails?" asked John. "On Wednesday?"

"I just wanted to see Leroy tackle a lobster tail before I die," Margaret giggled. "And no bibs in this establishment either."

Leroy's dark eyes smoldered. "You'll pay for this later," they seemed to say, but she didn't care. She could afford to taunt him. She was through with him after tonight. Any talk in town about her would soon die down, and in six months no one would remember that there once had been talk. There was no proof. Nobody had seen anything because there hadn't been anything to see.

He had a terrible time with the lobster, though *they* seemed to have just the right technique.

Later, after John had gone upstairs to work, they moved out to the porch. She turned to him, laughing in his face, chucking him under the chin. "That lobster was too much for you, eh?"

He put his arms around her, buried his face in the soft warmth of her throat and heard with pleasure the sharp intake of her breath. She made a pretext of struggling at first, but he took her small chin in the span of his thumb and forefinger and directed her parted lips, dry with desire, so subtly to seek and brush across his own that she did not suspect it was not her own inclination. She sank back, weak and trembling, to decide what to do. He gathered her hand to his mouth and nibbled tenderly on each of the tiny pads of her fingertips. She nuzzled at his ear, let him encircle her in his arms, her decision ("just once; just this once!") made, her resolutions shattered.

"Will you walk with me to the top of the steps?" His voice was thick, yet tender, she thought. He meant the winding S of steps leading from her garden up the hillside to the wood road. She nodded mutely, ready to go anywhere, do anything. Her only fear, now that she had committed herself, was that he would back out. Hand in hand, they tiptoed off the porch and walked awkwardly, their steps not yet attuned, across the driveway. As they crossed the moonless lawn, she caught a glimpse of Mrs. Haskell at the kitchen window and laughed to herself to have so easily eluded the woman's vigilant eye.

The May fragrances of fertile earth and honeysuckle swelled into headiness by the evening's warmth wafted toward them and served to guide them toward the steps, now half-hidden in the rampage of spring vines. They hesitated at the foot of the steps.

"Would you rather go back?" he asked timorously. "We could."

But she had decided. She had raised his hopes—she would go through with it. "Of course not," she whispered. "I want to." He kissed her on the cheek. "The female of the species has all the guts," she thought. She gave him her hand and let him lead her upward.

A sparkle of fireflies lit up the velvet darkness of the night, but the only sounds were nesting birds and their own footsteps. He stopped to hold a branch aside for her as they reached the grassy landing at the top of the steps but let it snap back too soon. It caught in her hair. His proximity as he reached to unsnarl it nearly made her swoon. Behind them lay the silent lawn and, beyond it, the river, its expanse of mystery and blackness interrupted only by the luminous bridge. As they watched, a nightliner from New York bound for Albany steamed into view, its triple tiers of light as it churned slowly through the inky water reminding her of the *bateaux mouches,* brilliant, gay, eternal, that she had watched on the Seine all those summers.

A rustle in the underbrush, followed by what sounded like a fine shower of gravel, startled her. "What was that?" she whispered fearfully, looking over her shoulder.

"A squirrel," he said, "or plums falling."

"There are no plums in May," she giggled nervously.

"It was nothing." He tried to slide his arm around her waist, but she eluded him. The sound had stirred up her apprehensions. She leaned against a tree instead, attributing her fears to a guilty conscience. Ten feet above, the guard rails along the wood road glowed in the darkness. For a few seconds she stood apart from him, inviolate, almost forgetting he was there, alive only to the beauty of the night, to the bridge far below, to the twinkling towns across the river. But as her eyes became accustomed to the pitchy darkness of the little woods, her attention turned to him and she could see the desire, undisguised and unmistakable, on his face. He stepped toward her and thrust himself at her willing body. She opened herself to his thrust and returned the kiss.

They separated breathlessly. "I want you," she whispered. His hands wandered over her body, and she was conscious only of her desire to lie down with him somewhere. They drew together again and were about to kiss when suddenly they were flooded with light. They leaped apart, blinded by the terrifying brilliance. With the instincts of a wild beast caught in a snare, she cried out, but from her trap, the cruel circle of light, there was no release.

Above, beyond the guard rails, low laughter and scuffling preceded a volley of catcalls and hoots.

"Get much, Le—roy?"

"Give it to her, Leroy baby!"

"Screw!"

"Screw, Marjie!"

"Atta boy, Leroy!"

A scrambling on the hillside, snickering, hushed whispers ("let's cut out, man"), a shower of gravel, and then, just as suddenly as it had appeared, the light disappeared. Car doors slammed. Motors were gunned, revved, raced. A final door was slammed; a final hoot, a final obscenity hurled, and the unmufflered cars roared away, leaving her alone in the darkness.

She called out for Leroy but he too had disappeared. There

was nothing and no one to comfort her. She whimpered softly to herself and called him again, hopelessly, then turned and hurried down the steps. The evening had grown cold. The gay nightliner had passed from sight and a lone car threaded its way across the bridge. She tripped and slid on the wet vines, but somehow reached the bottom of the steps without falling.

She started over the wet, slippery lawns, her only impetus the solitude of her bedroom and the oblivion of sleep. On the porch a tall figure moved, fumbled with a flashlight, walked down the porch steps and over the lawn toward her. Immobile she waited with head averted for his light to pick her out.

"Margaret? Is that you? What are you doing? What was all that noise?"

She could not make the muscles of her mouth function. She dropped helplessly to her knees on the grass.

"What are you doing?" He was upon her, paralyzing her with his light.

"I dropped my bracelet," she said numbly. "Here it is." Cumbrously she rose from the wet grass and faced him. Their feet were grounded in the pool of yellow light, their faces made grotesque by its refraction.

"Did you hear all that noise? Horns and motors and shouting?"

She fought back her nausea with a great effort. "I heard something, but it was way up on the road," she said faintly.

"I wonder what it was." He took her arm and turned her toward the house. "Where's Leroy?" he asked.

"Leroy? Why, he's gone. He left not long after you went upstairs."

"Oh."

She shivered uncontrollably, and he put his arm around

her to warm her. "Don't catch cold now," he said, half supporting her, half leading her, to the house.

"I won't." She strove to still her chattering jaws, but through the tears that stood in her eyes she could see their blazing castle of a house looming just ahead, each light waiting to discover on her face the knowledge in her heart.

A Note About the Author

Firth Haring was born in Tappan, New York. She attended public schools in Nyack, New York, and graduated from Barnard College. While at Barnard, she was awarded the Columbia University Press Prize for her news stories and drama reviews in the campus newspaper. Her junior year was spent at the University of London. Since graduation, she has worked for various publishing houses in New York; currently she is an Associate Editor in Harper & Row's College Department. Miss Haring is married to a businessman and has a baby daughter.